NEMIA RISING
EPISODE 1
TWIN DRAGONS WAKE

BY

JOSEPH A. DATTILO

Date Palm Press

First Edition: December 2017
ISBN: 978-1-948414-01-2

Author: Joseph A. Dattilo

Cover Design: Katherine Dattilo & Joseph A. Dattilo

Special Thanks to: Christopher O'Keefe, Katherine Dattilo, Bobby Williams, and everyone else who helped me get to this point.

Distributed by Date Palm Press™, a Date Palm Media LLC division.

This book is dedicated to my amazing wife, Katherine Dattilo, and my two boys, Vincent and Leonardo, without whom none of my efforts in this or anything else would have any meaning.

To my dear friend Christopher O'Keefe,

The worlds we created together and those characters who have been, once were, and have yet to be brought to life are largely a result of the long hours we spent as children imagining them into being.

This series would not have been possible without the many nights we toiled, hoping that one day each of our characters could finally come into being.

I know it's not a video game like we thought it would be, but I have a feeling someone reading this might be willing to work on fixing that some day.

P.S. Don't forget to nag me about the next book (often).

Sincerely,
Joseph Dattilo

To all who helped me get this far,

Thank you all for your encouragement and help along the way. I don't think I could have done this without each of you driving me to the finish line.

With the many years it has taken to get this far, I hope you all still agree that it was worth the wait and effort to finally be able to read the finished piece.

P.S. Don't forget to nag me about the next book (often).

Sincerely,
Joseph Dattilo

To You,

Thank you from the bottom of my heart for supporting my work. I like you. You are clearly an amazing person with impeccable taste in reading material, and I am lucky to be able to count you among my readers.

Right now, you are helping my dream of bringing the worlds and characters in my mind to life. Right this very moment, we have begun a journey together that I expect to be absolutely glorious, so please turn the page and enjoy the story.

P.S. Don't forget to nag me about the next book (often). Yeah, you thought you were off the hook ... sorry.

Sincerely,
Joseph Dattilo

NEMIA RISING EPISODE 1

TWIN DRAGONS WAKE

A RIDDLE IN THE NIGHT

Now how, might you ask, did the world as we know it come into being? What is the true tale behind the riddles of our past? I dare say, I am uniquely qualified to tell you this tale. And so, like it or not, I will.

Let me see ... where to begin? Well, a man sat in his office restlessly fidgeting with several small brightly shining metal orbs that rang softly in his calloused hands. His hands were not at all what one would expect of a well-to-do type. The spheres spun with dazzling speed between his long slender fingers, which moved with a surprising finesse.

Though he technically had no need to study war, magic, or anything else for that matter, he was easily bored and needed something to occupy his time. Today, he was struck particularly by how dull everything seemed. He felt his eyes were on the verge of popping out of his skull to find somewhere more interesting to live. Well ... that is what he imagined, at the time, was about to happen.

The nightmare had come again that night, the one where his father walked out the door for the last time, just like on that fateful day long past. Being a dream, though, that was where the similarity to reality always ended. Tonight, as the door closed, he had attempted to run and open it behind his father, for a change. Unfortunately, the door knob went missing before he could get there, and then the whole mansion had been consumed by a dreadful dull white light.

He had wandered around in the dream, hoping maybe something else would happen, but instead he just ended up sitting for what seemed ages, wondering when the god-awful thing was going to be over. Thankfully, when the dull white light had begun to consume him as well, he had been sufficiently terrified to awaken in a cold sweat.

The office he now sat in was brimming with contraptions and trophies of all sorts, though not much of anything in it was really his. And having never really felt it was his own, he avoided the study whenever possible. The place reminded him of his father, his father's father, and the sad reality of their absence. He did not understand, exactly, why he had, after all these years, decided to come here, but now that he was here he was struck by how much smaller his father's chair seemed. Though, happily, the room still smelled of familiar strong spirits and smoke, which momentarily reminded him of the awe with which he had once been filled as he watched his father from just around the corner of the door frame.

He scratched at his sideburns and puzzled over the papers and scattered diagrams that lay on every surface. They still lay as they had been, except for the dust and cobwebs that now clung greedily to them, untouched since the day of the disappearance.

He looked down, and the orbs came to a sudden stop in his hands. He had just remembered his father telling him proudly what they had been used for. He dropped them in disgust, and the loud clang rang ominously through the room as it broke the eerie silence, if only for a moment.

He wiped his hands on the inside of his jacket, and, once entirely certain that his dinner would stay where he had put it, he picked up an illustrative diagram of a peculiar circular device that looked like it was designed to hold seven spheres of some sort, with a much smaller slot in the center that was wide and tapered to a point on either side. Stroking his short, graying goatee, he wondered why so many of the diagrams seemed incomplete; practically none of them were even labeled.

"What in the world were you working on, Father?" he muttered under his breath as he shook his head, perplexed. His thick mane of brilliant auburn curls was hardly stirred by the motion. He did not know why, but the device seemed oddly familiar ... *Perhaps we already made th—* His train of thought was interrupted by a loud knocking on the door. Startled, he quickly pulled his feet off the table over which they had previously draped most unceremoniously. In the process, he sent several piles of diagrams flying. Cursing under his breath in Neichepan, he took a moment to regain his composure. "Who is it?" he shouted, his voice a little louder than necessary.

"I am dreadfully sorry, sir ... you ... uh, have a visitor, sir," came the youthful voice of the ever-bewildered and meek Matilda Vanna. A member of the manor's staff, Matilda would have been fired long ago, if it weren't for how much her master enjoyed watching her as she bent over, picking up after him day in and day out.

"A visitor?! I remember no arrangement for a visitor today." This was quite unusual, and as such, his tone was a strange combination of wary and curious, which led Matilda to one of the more uncomfortable silences that often struck her. It had been some time since a visitor had decided to grace him with their presence so late in the night. "And who, Matilda dear, might I ask ... wishes to visit me? I am a very busy man." This, of course, was a lie, as he was not busy at all. Well, at least, he hadn't been before the papers had exploded all over the floor.

He thought, "I suppose even another vagrant wanting a piece of my fortune must surely be better than this endless boredom."

"Sir, it is Chancellor Thanloa with an important message." The meek Matilda was likely regretting having interrupted her master's studies. He was always so busy, after all.

With a sigh, he said, "I suppose I can spare a few moments. Escort him to the gardens." He had been picking up the diagrams from the floor until he heard mention of the chancellor. If Thanloa had traveled all this way, there was little chance it was for a good game of Yeg Oh Na'yeg. Politicians, he had found, rarely came to play any games except those that involved his money, and it was even rarer that they brought good news. After all, "no news is good news" had been Thanloa's response to Gandora's question along those lines the last time he had visited. Gandora had not been thrilled to hear that a wild flock of birds had escaped from the local zoo. The massive ietqoo logiesen had ravaged several farms, and it apparently was considered his responsibility because his family had donated the cursed things in the first place. It was his opinion that people had grown to depend far too much on his and his family's goodwill.

Gandora slowly made his way to the gardens through the numerous archways and halls of his manor, walls covered with the portraits of the many, many Olaps who had preceded him. He had never felt comfortable in the extensive halls, with all the long-since-dead faces staring at him; the passages were far too dark, but he had never had the heart to change this. Superstition was uncharacteristic of him, but apparently, he made an exception for matters of décor for some reason.

He pushed open the towering doors that led to the manor gardens. Their weight was immense, and he was reminded of how proud he had been, as a child, on the day he first managed to make them budge. The thick steel beams of the massive portcullis that hung above his head still seemed to him as eternal and immovable as the sun and stars in the sky. He stepped out into the garden, the four moons overhead tonight making it brighter than usual.

Realizing how late it was, he grew much more concerned about the visit as he made his way to the fountain that glinted gently in the distance. Light shimmered on the bright green robes that surely belonged to Chancellor Thanloa.

The chancellor stood peering into the depths of the fountain, watching a group of curiously bright violet ut'thack fish swim in and out from behind the rocks that lay at the bottom. Several times he saw something serpentine dancing dangerously close to the large menacing teeth of the ut'thack. Any one of them would happily have eaten practically anything that fit in their mouths, and yet, somehow, they seemed unaware of the meal that lay so near them.

Thanloa guessed that they would have no problem with a worm of that size, which served only to puzzle him further as he waited impatiently in the brisk air of the ancient Olap gardens. In fact, looking at their large sharp teeth, he backed several paces away as he wondered, with good reason, whether it was particularly smart of him to stand as near as he did.

"I see you have found my ut'thack fountain. Lovely creatures, wouldn't you agree?" As Gandora said this, one of the ut'thack jumped a foot in the air, snatching a large glowing insect as it flew too low over the fountain.

Thanloa gasped in surprise as the insect's squeal of terror was suddenly cut short by the splashing of water and the sounds of its foot-long wings being ripped violently from its torso as several neighboring ut'thack took their part of the prize. Soon all that was left was a green cloud that spread an eerie glow across the water's surface.

Gandora came into view, beaming with pride as he watched his pets. He was wearing a colorful vest, fitting of his position, and held in his hand a golden walking stick that nicely matched his dark, gold-threaded slippers.

"Yes … umm … lovely." Thanloa cringed as the memory of the creature's death cry sent shivers down his spine. "Good evening, Master Olap," the chancellor said, in the most appealing tone he could manage.

"No good news for me, I presume?" Gandora's voice was stern but also revealed a hint of jest.

"Well, sir, let us say, neither good nor bad. In fact, I have little knowledge of … Well, that is, all I know is,

I promised your ... your father ..." his voice faltered, "I would entrust this to you, should the time come."

Thanloa awkwardly shoved his shaking right hand into a leather satchel that was draped over his shoulder. He pulled out an antique silver lockbox. The chancellor shoved the parcel unceremoniously into Gandora's hands. "He told me to tell you 'The Gate has awoken,'" he said with a shudder.

Though it was hard to tell in the shadows of the night, the unexpectedly heavy rounded box seemed to be embossed with strange symbols—symbols surprisingly unfamiliar to Gandora, despite his erudition.

"'The Gate has awoken'? And why, pray tell, would my father want you to tell me that?" Gandora was perplexed and a little annoyed. "What 'Gate' do you speak of? And what the hell is this?" He shook the box as he spoke, and its contents rapped dully inside.

"I have said too much already, I fear ..." The chancellor's voice was hushed; he looked around nervously, as if someone were listening in from the bushes.

Gandora was flummoxed; the chancellor never acted thusly. Generally, he came and barked orders as if he owned the place. Today, however, things seemed entirely different—completely out of character, in fact.

Muttering under his breath, Gandora let his gaze fall onto the box that now lay in his hands. The box glittered brightly as he pulled it out of the shadows and directly into the moonlight. He traced the strange symbols with his right index finger and grumbled unintentionally. Stooping down, he shook the box once more and listened intently to the strangely hollow sound it made.

When he lifted his eyes to where the chancellor had stood, he saw that he was gone, nowhere to be found. "More riddles! Figures that's all he would leave behind." He flung his walking stick several yards; somewhere in the dark, it slammed loudly into a tree.

He was overcome by a swirl of feelings: confusion, loneliness, a great uneasiness. He longed unexpectedly for the boredom he had known only moments ago, before Thanloa's arrival; he fumed at the enigma in his hands.

Had he known then what he would learn later, he would have tried to give it back or locked it away in the deepest recesses of the manor.

But, I have not set out to tell you what could have been, so let us continue in the telling of what was. I would like to believe that it all began in a place as familiar as I have just described, but alas, believing so would not make it any more the truth. Let us go, then, to a far different place, and a slightly different time, so that you might better understand those things that later came to pass.

A DIFFERENT WORLD

If only one could have seen in so lightless a vacuum as that pitch-black studio apartment; if they could have, they would have beheld what might have been one of the most immaculate, and sparsely decorated, rooms imaginable. The room was not more than nine cubits long by eight cubits wide, and its only furnishings were the tiny fold-out desk that clung desperately to the wall and a lonely futon, upon which a man now quietly lay.

It was not exactly what one would expect of a young man's residence; it was, however, just the type of place one could expect this particular twenty-six-year-old to call home.

Kumogami Katsumoto, who then went by Kumo, lay in the dark looking up at the ceiling and watching the distortions that formed in his vision as he stared too long. He liked it in his dark, quiet sanctuary. In fact, he preferred darkness in general and, if given the choice, would never go out during the day.

It was almost sunset, so for Kumo it was about time to get up. Kumo was a graduate student in archeology and took classes at night. Whenever his schedule allowed it, he also worked as a part-time night watchman (which is a fancy way of saying he was a security guard) at the public library. He encountered few people during his rounds at the library, and his classes tended to be rather small, so his contact with other humans, and thus the amount he seemed to trouble them, was kept to a minimum.

With a long sigh, he rolled off the futon and began to fold it up. He slid it into the corner to the right of the entryway of his tiny kitchen. Standing up, he made his way to the front door and flipped a switch. Moments later, a gentle red glow filled the room.

He stepped toward the sturdy silver machine that lay in solitude atop the tiny fold-out desk. I am told that the device is called a "laptop." The best I can describe it is to say that it is similar to a handheld but is larger, bulkier, and certainly more primitive, but I digress. He opened its lid and pushed the power button. After a short chorus of hums and whirrs, the laptop came to life.

It was not long before the sounds of a cello quartet playing Pachelbel's Canon in D Minor slowly filled the apartment. (I find it unlikely that you would know of Pachelbel, but, in the land of which I speak, his compositions have long been celebrated.) One might never have guessed that they were in the middle of a giant downtown metropolis by the eerie quiet that had just been shattered by mere memories of gentle bow strokes across instrument strings.

Kumo had replaced the apartment's carpet with several layers of cushy black soundproofing floor mats. The walls, ceiling, even the doors were covered in acoustic soundproofing foam. It was difficult to tell where exactly they were, but several speakers had been mounted strategically throughout the tiny space.

As the speakers filled the room with the slowly growing melody, Kumo made his way into the kitchen. Hung over the sink, from several wires, was a collection of photographs. Nineteen in all, they depicted an eighth-century Islamic vase that had recently been found in the location of the former Heijokyo Palace, Japan.

He had been lucky enough to be on the expedition that dug up the pieces, and he had taken the photographs at his first opportunity. It looked like they had finished developing. He checked to make sure that the lids were still sealed on the two pails of developing chemicals that sat in the corner to his left. Then, carefully, he unclipped each of the photographs from the wires, stacking them neatly in a little pile in front of him.

Before leaving the room, Kumo placed a small pot of water on the stove, turned the burner's knob to high, and wiped down the sink. On his way out, he flipped another switch on the wall. The eerie red glow that had filled the room instantly disappeared, and as his eyes adjusted he was able to catch the slightest hint of a fading red glow that emanated from the cooling coils in the bulbs. He flipped another switch, and with a buzz and a moment's pause the whole room was filled with heavily diffused fluorescent light.

He slunk into the bathroom. It offered only a small closet, a toilet, and a tiny shower stall. Quickly he exchanged his current adornments with an identical set he pulled from the closet. Moments later, after finishing the tying and tucking of his black leather bootlaces, he checked himself over in the tiny mirror above the sink.

His hair was a stream of silver mercury that poured down from atop his head in the reflection before him. The contrast it made with his unnaturally pale skin was startling. Below the sleek silver, his eyes were as pink windows into his soul. Few looked into them; they were too unnerving. There was a fierce drive in them that was both beautiful and frightening.

He hadn't been given a choice in the matter of his birth as an albino, but he was determined not to let that fact stop him from reaching his goals in life. Still, it hadn't exactly given him a leg up as an archaeologist. People tended to be too distracted by the condition to pay attention to the person. Even worse was the type of welcome a "red-eyed demon" received when visiting Third World countries for a dig.

Despite popular belief, the genetic mutation does not strip albinos of the ability to spend time in the sun. That said, there were still lines on his face from a particularly bad sunburn from a dig long past. Kumo's dislike for gawking crowds, however, provided the bulk of the reason for him to keep his schedule of events to the night. Even if it was mostly the memories of his childhood that really kept him inside, he was sure little could have changed from then to now.

He strained to read the time from a clock that hung at the opposite end of the apartment. He gave up, not bothering to walk the six paces it would have taken to make an accurate reading of it. His vision was poor in comparison to that of those who had normal eyes, but he felt he more than made up for it with his superb hearing. Sadly, having good ears had only meant he had been blessed from a young age with the ability to hear gasps of shock from a greater distance.

He made his way back into the kitchen, where the water was now at a boil. He pulled a package of instant miso soup from the cupboard and ripped it open, pouring its contents into the water. He liked miso soup, but though he naturally preferred it fresh, he was sadly lacking in the domestic skills required to make it himself, despite no lack of means to purchase the ingredients. So, he made do by trying his best to ignore the texture of the recently rehydrated seaweed as it slid slimily over his tongue.

Now he reserved his focus for the examination of the photographs that lay before him. By and large, they had turned out as well as he could have hoped for, considering the hurried nature of their taking.

He would enjoy researching the vase's origins later tonight. Working as a security guard at a library offered him almost as much peace and quiet as his own little sanctuary did. Additionally, it provided something that his apartment could never have offered—thousands of years of knowledge passed down through generations. Being paid to spend countless nights among texts both yellowed by age and those so fresh from the presses that they had never felt a human hand was, to say the least, a happily received bonus. Not to mention the time that the job offered for completing his studies.

He turned off the stove and poured his soup into a small bowl. After he had finished scooping the last bits of seaweed and tofu into his mouth, he quickly washed the dish and pot, leaving them to dry on the counter.

He pulled on his black trench coat and made his way to the door. The fact that, at this time of day, few were concerned with his choice of attire certainly did nothing to detract from the advantages of life by night. On his way out, he hit the power button to his computer, it whirred violently, and then suddenly there was utter silence. The neat pile of photographs in hand, he turned out the apartment lights and reached for the door.

As the door opened, the world outside screamed to life, full of sights, sounds, and smells. The sour odor of rotting natto wafted in from the small shops that lined the street (a wretched waste of a good batch of beans, if you ask me). In the same burst of air came a handful of more pleasant but less powerful odors whose origins were less easily distinguished. The hum and bustle of the busy downtown Tokyo streets ripped through the air in an almost deafening blast.

For a moment, it seemed as if the world would tear the room apart, its essential nature in perfect opposition to its surroundings. Yet as soon as the feeling had begun, it was already over. Kumo quickly slipped out into the street and, with a certain finality, turned the key, locking the door behind him. The room again was filled with a dark silence. The world that only moments before had seemed an unstoppable force was once again held at bay. The sanctuary would wait patiently for its master's return.

INTOXICATING ENCHANTRESS

A cab stopped in the middle of a chaotic Tokyo street. Moments later, its rear door opened, and two smooth long legs gracefully slid out. The owner of those long legs was a tall, caramel-toned woman wearing a short, brilliant white skirt paired with silver stilettos. Her hot pink–and–orange silk chiffon halter top billowed in the afternoon breeze, revealing her well-toned midriff. The raven-colored hair that wrapped elegantly atop her head glinted and gleamed, the intricately woven updo hiding the tops of her ears. The tightly wound bun ended at the back of her head with nine long, lavishly curling strands that extended past her shoulders gliding effortlessly behind her.

She wasn't sure exactly what had made her choose to visit Japan; the trip was just a whim she'd followed through on. She felt as though, in the grand scheme of things, all she was capable of doing anymore was wasting time being bored by the prospect of another day. As far as she was concerned, it mattered little whether she spent her time bored in Japan, England, or any other place, so even if nothing came of the visit, it was hardly a loss.

She spied the establishments before her and, in a moment, found her quarry. It was getting late in the afternoon, and she needed a drink ... or two.

As she thrust open the bar's old rickety door, gray smoke billowed out, carrying with it the sweet smell of sake and the familiar odor of many drunken men. It was dark inside, and shadows danced on the walls as she sauntered through the thick clouds that filled the room.

Soon she found herself standing in front of an elderly gentleman who was rather as unkempt as the bar was. He gaped at her, clearly befuddled by her stunning presence in his ratty bar. Though she couldn't see it, he pinched his arm, trying to confirm whether he had drunk himself into unconsciousness yet. As the sweet smell of lilies penetrated the musty air, he shook his head, trying to clear away the accompanying stupor that engulfed him.

After it seemed to him years had passed, his head finally cleared, and he was able once again to form words. As he stared into the woman's enchanting emerald eyes, he choked out, "And, uh—how, uh, Miss, can I-I help you?"

ΔΔΔ

Meanwhile, outside the bar, Kumo passed through the clouds of smoke that billowed out of its decrepit doors. Making no attempt to hide his disgust for the noxious fumes, he hurried down the street, holding his breath until the air had cleared. The plumes of smoke had dissipated to tiny wisps in the wind. He inhaled air that now stank only of natto and that hint of smog that he could never quite escape. Continuing on his way to the train station at the street's end, he wished, as he often did, that he lived somewhere else entirely.

It was an uncomfortable trip; it always was. Some nights, passengers were crammed so tightly that they practically sat on each other's laps. Comparatively, tonight was a good night. He was still pressed tightly between two elderly women who bickered through him, as though he wasn't even there. But though they argued quietly over who was older the whole way to Chiyoda, a province of Tokyo, Kumo was so delighted by the entire three inches of clearance that lay spaciously before him that he barely even noticed.

At his stop, he slowly edged out through the crowds making his way to the street, where he continued his trek to Sophia University on foot.

The Social Sciences building appeared to be a white block, lined with the tiny gray squares that were its windows. It loomed behind several more attractive buildings, looking a little out of place. Among the more notable edifices was a large cylindrical brick building, sitting comfortably at the edge of the curb. He had never been inside it, but he had always admired its craftsmanship. Alas, today would be no different from any other day. He passed the building and made his way up into the sample preparation and storage area.

Tonight, his labor was not unlike that of most graduate students; he was basically doing grunt work for a professional who worked in the field that he hoped to pursue one day, and tuition had him paying for the privilege. He made his way quickly through the halls to the storage rooms. Upon arriving, he pulled off his trench coat, hanging it over the corner of a tall shelf. From the shelf, he pulled a box that was labeled "P-31." Setting the box on a well-lit desk, he sat and began to carefully clean the delicate pieces of pottery stowed inside it. It was time-consuming and tedious work, but work that needed doing. By two in the morning, the pieces were looking very nice. He would have loved to finish them tonight, but not wanting to risk his security job, he knew it was time to go.

Kumo had applied to work for the National Diet Library because it was the largest library in Japan. Of course, the fact that it was the only library used for the Japanese legislature, and consequently the only library that had a persistent need for security guards at night, may also have contributed to his choice.

Kumo took the twelve-minute journey, only four minutes of which were spent on the train, and settled into his post.

ΔΔΔ

As Kumo scoured over ancient Islamic texts, the tall black-haired woman still sat in the shabby old bar in downtown Tokyo.

Her table was in the far corner. She dipped her finger in a cup of nihonshu, a strong Japanese sake, and stirred it gently. It had been served hot, and though it wasn't the highest quality stuff, it certainly got the job done.

She paused, wondering if perhaps she had overdone it tonight, but then reconsidering, she downed her drink in one gulp. Sweat dripped from her brow. Ventilation in the bar was terrible. Her vision blurred, and the world seemed to press heavily upon her shoulders. She'd lost count of the drinks that continued to make their way to her. All she knew was that, at least for the moment, the thirst that consumed her seemed quenched. Maybe she could close her eyes for just for a moment ... a moment couldn't hurt.

ΔΔΔ

The barkeep looked up at the clock, 3:29 am. Time to close up shop for the night, and only one customer left. To his surprise, he found that customer to be the beautiful woman who had stolen his breath earlier. She lay passed out at the table, one hand tightly grasping a bottle of sake, the other sprawled limply next to an overturned cup whose contents had begun to dribble over the table's edge.

He didn't have the heart to wake her, so, after wiping up the mess, he simply threw a blanket over her shoulders. Then, he locked the doors and made his way upstairs to his bedroom. He wouldn't normally allow a passed-out customer to spend the night, but he was certain she wouldn't stir 'til morning. And, after all, she would be much safer kept off the streets in her present condition.

A SOBERING SIGHT

She had closed her eyes for only a moment, but when she opened them again the bar was empty. Her face ached, probably because she'd spent the night facedown on the table. She could see where her drool had puddled and dried. Her hand still clung to the bottle of sake, and an old worn quilt was wrapped over her shoulders.

As she stood, a terrible pain shot up her spine and into her head. "You've really outdone yourself this time," she thought. Despite the agony, she was able to make her way to the door.

She would rather have liked to thank the barkeep but thought better of waiting around any longer. Dropping a thick wad of cash behind the bar on her way, she unlocked the door and slipped outside.

Bright daylight and loud bustling streets greeted her, burning her skull as if it were aflame. She had developed a habit of drinking like this. Hung over wasn't her favorite way to wake up, but at least she had slept in relative peace.

She walked down the street in no particular direction, hoping to find somewhere quiet where she could slowly acclimate to being among the living again. Eventually she came upon a small coffee shop; it looked peaceful enough. She stepped in, and the bell on the door rang out. Oh god, her head! She paused, grimacing until the waves of pain, dizziness, and nausea passed, then pulled herself together and made her way to the end of the short line.

Whether by fate, or dumb luck, Kumo also found himself in the quaint, corner coffee shop. Not ready to finish his research for the night, he'd settled comfortably into a large leather loveseat, sipping at his coffee and reading Ibn Fadlan's account of the Rus, which had been written by the Arabic chronicler in the year 921 C.E. (which stands for Common Era and is used as a date reference system of sorts). He hoped to find some clue as to how the vase had ended up in the country a century earlier than known history allowed for. So far it was an intriguing read, but he had made little progress in finding an answer.

The girl ordered her coffee and a glass of water. The smell of the place had already begun to clear her head, something she was certainly glad for. The shop was cute; she loved that the walls were covered with pictures of its customers. The Polaroids were gathered in little bunches here and there, adding to the eclectic style of the establishment. Surveying the room, she noticed some rather comfortable-looking couches inviting customers to stay a while.

She made her way eagerly to the nearest open spot and happily sunk into the cushions. It was a delightful feeling, like a deep embrace. Sleeping on the table last night had left her with an awful crick in her neck. She would have to put more thought into finding a comfortable place to rest tonight ... perhaps somewhere with an open bar. Just the thought made her stomach churn, but not enough to change her mind.

Kumo looked up as the girl walked by and flopped herself into the chair next to his. The sweet smell of lilies and the unmistakable waft of sake drifted to him, not the most pleasant combination as they mingled in his nostrils. He thought about moving but decided that it wasn't bad enough to warrant the distraction. (This was a decision that he would later come to regret.) He continued reading, particularly enjoying the likely exaggerated account of the disgusting bathing habits of the Rus. Soon his ears were greeted by the sounds of his neighbor's eager slurping.

She tossed the empty cup, annoyed by its blatant disregard for her unceasing thirst. It sailed effortlessly over the strangely pale man who sat next to her and landed perfectly in the trash. She stood up with whatever little grace she could muster as she hurried to the ladies' room, failing only slightly to stride with ladylike purpose as the "urgent matter" that had come to her bladder's attention became increasingly urgent with each step she took.

Kumo was relieved to see her go. Maybe she wouldn't come back. "Now, where was I?" he whispered to himself. He had got to the part of the narrative that told of the Rus king and the four hundred servants who had gladly allowed themselves to be buried at his side and hoped that this too was an exaggeration or misinterpretation of what had really transpired.

Buried in his book, Kumo had not noticed that his neighbor had returned. He turned his head, and, to his surprise, her face was only inches from his. She lay across the two couches, propping her head up with one hand and holding another cup of coffee in the other. Her face had brightened noticeably, and it looked as though she had done something with her hair. Briefly, it struck Kumo that she was quite beautiful ... until, again, she slurped loudly in his ear, which reminded him of her other qualities.

Apparently, she hadn't been satisfied by the first cup and hadn't bothered to consider whether her slurping was disturbing anyone. She had, however, noticed the apparent age of the book he read, and, having taken care of her bodily needs as much as she could, she was inclined to satisfy her curiosity. "Whatcha readin'?" she asked in the cutest voice she could manage. She was even more intrigued now that she could see why the man was so pale.

Kumo had been wondering if he shouldn't have found another spot, or maybe another coffee shop, when she interrupted his train of thought. "This? Oh, just an old book. You wouldn't know it," he said with unwavering certainty. He was annoyed. Why on earth was this girl talking to him? The only girls who ever talked to him were covered in piercings and tattoos, and she had none (that he could see). Futhermore, she looked too young to be interested in him—she couldn't be a day over twenty-three.

She, however, seemed extremely insulted by his assumption. "Try me!" she exclaimed, with a hint of fierceness in her tone that had not been there before.

He decided to humor the girl. After all, she would leave him be when she heard what he was reading. Citing an ancient Islamic chronicler was a tried-and-true way to make people lose interest in his company. "It is called the Risala. Now—"

"I knew it!" She looked as if she were posing for the victory snapshot after having defeated a bear in hand-to-hand combat. "Why are you reading that confounded Ibn Fadlan's rubbish?" Kumo sensed that, beneath her sense of triumph, she was genuinely concerned by his choice of authors.

Kumo, who could have sworn he had mentioned nothing of Ibn Fadlan, puzzled over the girl's eager face. He had never met anyone outside of academia who would have given two seconds to the work of Ibn Fadlan. Of course, it seemed that this girl was in agreement on that count, but the fact that she knew of the Risala left him in a perplexed silence.

She seemed to take the silence as permission to continue. "I am personally more a fan of the work of Masoudi. His accounts were much less ... *biased*. Then again, Ibn Fadlan's stuff was more entertaining, if that's what you're after. Don't you think?" She paused, waiting for his response.

He still sat stunned, staring blankly into her eyes, his brow occasionally twitching.

After waiting for what she figured was long enough, she edged back abashedly. "Oh, sorry. I suppose it's unlikely you would have read Masoudi's work ..." Her heart sank, as her hope for a good conversation suddenly died.

"No. No, I have, Miss, it's just ... I never expected to meet anyone else who had." He felt bad for making her doubt herself, but he was genuinely surprised and at a loss for words. His mind was busy trying to make sense of his current situation and not a lot of it was left to devote to socializing, a skill that didn't come naturally to him.

Her disappointment suddenly vanished, and she pulled her face even closer to his. "Which are your—" A glint of something amber caught her eye.

All time stopped. She leaned in, staring at the source of her entrancement. Her mind cleared, and she no longer felt the throb of pain in her brow. The ring was much cleaner than the last time she had seen it. She moved closer, her nose almost touching it. The fragments of color in the stone seemed alive as she edged forward, watching them change slightly in hue. How had she not noticed this before?

"Umm ... Miss?" Kumo was feeling several degrees more embarrassed than he had ever felt in all his years as she had slowly crawled her way even closer. She was perched precariously, one hand gripping his thigh, which was as far as he was prepared to let it creep.

"Huh?" Her concentration broken, she looked up at him, puzzled. Her delicately balanced grip suddenly lost, she let out a squeal of surprise, falling headlong into his lap. She struggled in the fall, pulling forward just enough to avoid absolute disgrace. During the act, however, she felt a hard thud on her forehead and still found herself lying sprawled atop the man she had only just met.

"Are you okay?!" He was concerned about her face smashing into the edge of his book. His heart was racing; he had no idea what to do. He was not accustomed to women falling for him, whether or not it was in the literal sense. He also felt slightly ashamed that her lying sprawled where she did had made his pulse race and his breath bate more than anything else that thus far had transpired. Just thinking about it worried him even more as he felt an involuntary twitch.

For what felt a lifetime she lay there in his lap while his mind raced frantically, coming to no conclusion other than it was decisively not his place to take any further action. After all, nothing in his interactions with other women had adequately prepared him for this moment. Had she not just ruined his previous distaste for her company, he likely would have simply shoved her away. Instead, in however many seconds had passed with her face firmly planted in his crotch, he had gone through at least a hundred scenarios where this could not possibly end well for him and about a half dozen where they ended even worse.

Finally, she turned over, reaching her hand instinctively to her forehead, as the pain that had just left it came raging back threefold. She guessed she was bleeding without seeing any blood; her new friend had gone from a bright red flush to a shade of sickly pallor that seemed unnatural even for someone of his kind. She figured that this was partly due to where she had landed, but that couldn't explain the whole of his expression ... at least not in her experience.

"Is it that bad?" She would have believed anything, with the pain she felt.

"I d-don't know." He quickly pulled a pile of napkins from his coat pocket and placed it on her forehead.

"Oh my, am I bleeding?" she said in a convincingly distraught tone, though she now knew, as her pain subsided, that she would be fine. Having just taken in her present situation, she decided to enjoy herself. "Tell me! Is it bad?"

"Uh … yes. I mean, no. Well, err … there *is* blood, Miss, but I think it's not bad?" He peeked at the napkins and cringed at the small circle of blood that had soaked through the top. He really hoped his assessment was accurate. "I am so sorry, Miss. If there's anything I can do, anything at all …"

"There is, actually. I need to clean up, so lead the way."

"'Lead the way?' And, where exactly are we going?"

"Your place, silly!" She tried her best to bat her eyes with girlish charm. She felt like it wasn't coming across the way she had hoped, but she couldn't really be sure. Either way, she made a mental note to practice when she got the chance.

He had expected just about anything else, really, when he'd offered help. So, he once again stared at her blankly, not knowing what to do while he waited for some of the blood to return to his head.

"Come on! It is the least you can do for me, seeing how it was your book that did this." She pointed to her head, making a show of the pain she was in.

He thought about protesting but, catching another glimpse of blood, decided—whether or not it had been his fault—he was probably better off playing nice. "Fine."

Her face went from a pout to a giddy smile. "Okay, how far is it?"

"Just outside, actually."

"My name's Alison. You can call me Alice." She batted her eyes flirtatiously and felt much more satisfied with his response this time. "I've still got it!" she thought, absolutely preening at the success of her recovery.

"Uh, Kumo. Just *Kumo*." He sighed.

Alice's smile widened in spite of herself, and in moments she was on her feet, dragging Kumo by one hand.

Bewildered, he trailed behind her as he tried to figure out exactly how he found himself in this predicament.

ESSENTIALLY
UNINVITED

Alice's eyes widened in surprise. When Kumo opened his door, the dark nothingness that loomed beyond it filled her with a terrible unease. Maybe this hadn't been such a great idea after all.

"Here we are."

She was slightly relieved by the white light that filled the room when Kumo flipped a switch on the wall. Then, taking in the décor, or lack thereof, her relief vanished. "Oh, my! Who is your decorator? I must know!" She laughed nervously. She was starting to worry she had made a wrong choice in coming here.

"My decorator?" He was a bit perplexed by this question but answered as best he could. "I guess that would be me. Why, you like it?" He put his hands on his hips and proudly surveyed the room.

"Oh—" Alice thought for a moment; she should have guessed that his place might have a *unique* style from what he was wearing. "Yes, it is quite, um, … cavernous." She tried to make it sound like a compliment, keeping her tone ridiculously upbeat and shooting him a friendly smile. She hoped her cover-up would pass.

"I know! Isn't it great?!"

To her amazement, he was beaming with pride. Glad that his last question had been rhetorical, she made a mental note never to consult him in matters of interior design.

The strange man with flowing silver hair continued holding the door open. "So, are you coming in or what?" She took one last deep breath of the outside air and braved a step over the threshold.

Glorious silence fell over the room as Kumo shut the door, sealing out the world. The pain that burned through her skull dulled, and she decided—even if only for this—she was glad to be here, after all.

"I have a first aid kit over here." Kumo walked into the bathroom and pulled out a large camo bag from the bottom of the closet.

"I should consider myself lucky if he has anything in here at all. He seems a … minimalist at best," she thought, looking around as she made her way to him.

Kumo pulled out a bottle of isopropyl alcohol, a handful of cotton balls, antibacterial cream, and—after some thought—several butterfly bandages. He really hoped they wouldn't need more than that; he was concerned about whether he should have taken her to the hospital, hoping desperately he'd made the right judgment call.

Alice looked into the immense bag, which was likely one of the largest things in the small apartment. Inside there was a huge variety of emergency first-aid equipment ranging from the humble Band-Aid to what appeared to be a military-grade tourniquet and a pack of instant wound sealant. *What a surprise. Seems at least he is prepared for the apocalypse. Though what would*

*be the point of surviving if it meant living in this hole,
I don't know.*

He poured the alcohol on one of the balls of cotton and removed the napkins from her forehead. "I am … so sorry." He looked ashamed.

She could see now in the mirror that there was more blood than she had expected. It did not take long before it began to drip down onto her clothing. "Don't worry about it. I'm sure it will be fine."

"Ready? This'll sting a little."

She nodded gently and braced herself against the white countertop. As the cotton ball drew closer, the alcohol smell made her stomach lurch.

"Are you okay?"

"Oh, it's nothing!" Her face was pale; she was doing her best to keep her coffee down.

Once Kumo was satisfied that she was indeed all right, he continued. The sting, when it came, was not nearly as bad as what Alice had expected—not that she enjoyed it. Well, she didn't care for the pain part, at least. She was, however, thoroughly enjoying the attention.

He worked quickly, cleaning the wound thoroughly. When he had finished, Alice stared into the mirror. She would scarcely have believed her head had just been a bloody mess, except it still throbbed where the butterfly bandage now closed her cut. She was a little ashamed to admit she was disappointed he had finished so quickly.

"All done!" he said, tossing the blood-soaked cotton balls as he began putting away the rest of his supplies.

"Wow. Thanks!" She continued admiring his work until he had finished. Then, she somehow managed to squeeze herself to his other side; he held his breath as she brushed against him, suddenly aware of their proximity. Stuck in this awareness, he didn't realize that he was quickly being pushed out the door, until it was too late.

"What are you doing?" Kumo reached for the door, but it had already closed.

"Cleaning up. No peeking!"

Kumo heard the shower turn on and realized what she was doing. His adrenaline started pumping again as he heard her kicking off her stilettos. "Man, I am way too tired for this," he thought. He started to slide down the wall, but before he had reached the floor, the door creaked open an inch. His guest peeked out, a sliver of her creamy skin tantalizingly visible. This was doing things to him that he did not currently have the energy for.

"I almost forgot ... Kuuuvey, would you mind picking me up a new outfit?" She shoved a handful of money through the doorway.

"What about the one you had?" Kumo's brow twitched upon hearing her nickname for him.

"Oh, those old things? I tossed 'em."

"Tossed 'em?!" Kumo was pretty certain those clothes hadn't been terribly old, though they had reeked of cigarette smoke and alcohol.

"Well, they were *dirty*. Now, go be a dear and grab me something cute! Or do you think it would be decent to leave me stranded in here?"

Kumo was pretty certain she was right about it being rude to refuse a woman clothing, especially when she was naked in your bathroom.

"Now, I am a size 7, tall, and I want something pink."

"Why don't you just take them out of the trash?"

"Absolutely not! Now, go on. Get going. Oh, and could you be a dear and not pick the clothes

yourself? Ask someone at the store to do it, please."
Just then she had remembered his trench coat—
and his apartment.

"I have some clean clothes in the closet. Just wear them." She wasn't that much smaller than he was after all, but from the look of disgust he received, he guessed that it wasn't the size that she was concerned about. Clearly, logic wasn't going to work on this girl, so he carefully averted his eyes and reached over, blindly groping for the cash. After a moment, he had the money in hand.

"What the hell kind of woman carries cash like this?" Kumo muttered grumpily under his breath, still trying to wrap his dizzy head around her reasons for ridding herself of a perfectly good outfit as he edged toward the exit.

"Oh, and Kuvey dear! Do remember to pick up *everything* a girl needs." He was pretty sure he heard her trying—and failing—to stifle a giggle as the bathroom door shut firmly. He stepped outside, his face turning a bright red and his eyes widening as what she meant dawned on him.

Patting his left pocket as he went, he was relieved to hear the clamor of his keys as they beat against each other. He felt uncomfortable leaving this stranger in his apartment. However, that was the least of his worries as he set out on his mission, seeking something the likes of which he had never sought before.

Kumo ambled aimlessly through the crowded streets of downtown Tokyo, almost forgetting why he was there in the first place. This was exactly the time of day he preferred to be indoors. The crowds seemed to swell and charge at him from all directions, an illusion that was not diminished by the confused trance that sleeplessness had cast upon him.

Something that looked like a mannequin wearing a green feather boa and a leather jacket caught his eye, and somehow he managed to cut his way through the throng of pedestrians that blocked his path. After stumbling in, he slowly edged his way toward the counter. His eyes were half-closed, and his mouth hung open slightly. Just one more thing left to do …

Meanwhile, in the shower, the water was warm and soothing; it beat down in thick droplets that crashed pleasantly upon Alice's shoulders. This may have been the smallest shower she had ever seen, but somehow it still felt comfortable. This was definitely one of the "little things" in life she could appreciate.

She saw a worn bar of soap perched on the rack that hung beneath the showerhead. She almost reached for it, but stopped short just before she touched it. *Probably not a good idea*, she thought, as she looked around for something slightly less ... taintable.

There was some shampoo, which she figured was the best she would find. "Here goes nothing!" She took a deep breath and held it, dreading the musky smell that was sure to follow. A moment later, disturbingly bright fluorescent blue goo began to stream out from the overturned bottle. It pooled uncomfortably in a giant globule at the top of her crown.

This is definitely not the vacation I pictured. Not at all. She squeezed out the last from the bottle and tossed it callously to the shower's floor, making a small splash. She couldn't help but catch a whiff of the predictably musky sludge as she lathered up her hair. Luckily, the stuff rinsed off easily enough.

It was not until the water had long gone cold that she decided she may as well check on the boy's progress. She stepped out of the shower, quickly wrapping herself in a towel as the cold air engulfed her, sending goose bumps down her neck and arms. She cracked open the door as slightly as she could and peeked out through her still-dripping hair.

Kumo lay passed out against the wall next to a small pile of clothing. The first thing she noticed was the fuzzy pink slippers that lay atop the bundle, their floppy ears mocking her as she stared into their beady little eyes. She shuddered but deciding that she could make anything look good; she grabbed the clothes and scurried back to the privacy of the bathroom.

What greeted her was: a fuzzy pink turtleneck, pink sweatpants, long red-and-white striped socks, and, of course ... the bunny slippers. He hadn't forgotten her undergarments—little bouncing happy lop-eared bunnies covered every inch of them. *What was with him and the bunnies?!* Begrudgingly, she pulled on the outfit, which hung loosely over her shoulders, several sizes too large. She sincerely doubted that he had even made any effort to follow her instructions. She arranged her hair into its former style and made her way abashedly out of the bathroom.

Alice had been too busy to notice how tired the poor boy was, but watching as he lay slouched uncomfortably against the wall, his head bobbing slightly as he snored, she could tell it would be a while before he woke again. She quietly unrolled his futon next to him. He slid easily enough, as she gently pulled him down upon it. His head bounced slightly on the squishy surface, but he seemed none the worse for it, as he did not stir again until much later.

PRESUMPTOUS PRESENCE

Kumo lay curled comfortably on his futon. He dreamed he was reading something, but he couldn't tell what it was, as every time he started to get into it he was interrupted, again and again. It was a nightmare.

He still felt tired but found himself slowly drifting back into consciousness. It was a while before his senses began to recover, but when they did, he was sure he heard something that did not belong. A rhythmic clanking and rattling chorus echoed in his head. The noise seemed very far away, as if a part of his dreams. He ignored it and had almost drifted back to sleep when the clatter was spiked by harsh and jagged-sounding murmurs he could not ignore.

Oh, God! He sat up quickly, fearing the worst. He shot out of bed in an instant, his fists at the ready. He had taken only a few karate classes, but he hoped a good show of the little he had learned as a child would be enough to at least distract his assailant.

"Was für ein haufen scheiße!" Kumo could now clearly hear the sharp *tink* of glass against glass, accompanied by a guttural German accent, and a chill went up his spine as he approached the kitchen. *"Scheiße! Bumsen! Warum? Es ist die ganze scheiße!"*

Kumo stopped and almost retreated but quickly regained his composure and stormed into the kitchen. As he turned the corner, he saw two long and slender legs vanishing into a short black skirt sticking out from behind the open fridge door. There was another clang, and the angry voice rang out again: *"Ich hätte nie geschätzt! ... Ungültig!"* Two jars flew into the air, crashing loudly into the tall metal trash can that sat in the corner at the intruder's heels.

"Who the hell do you think you are?" Kumo's pumping adrenaline prepared him for just about anything at this point.

"Oh! Did I wake you?" The soft voice that fluttered gently into his ears was the last thing Kumo had expected, and thus he was not prepared. Alice was peeking her head over the edge of the open fridge, still crouched in front of it.

"Uh ... You think?"

At first there was a bright smile on her face, but it was quickly replaced by a grimace. "Is there any food in this dreadful hole that hasn't expired?!"

Kumo looked into the trash can that was now almost overflowing. He was pretty sure he didn't recognize anything in it. "Expired?"

"Yes, expired! EEE-EX-PEE-EYE-ARR-EEE-DEE! A word commonly used to refer to things that *kill* you when you eat them!" She tossed a jar of red and brown slime into the trash as she spoke; the label had said "olives," but she found it hard to believe that it had ever contained anything edible.

Kumo rarely opened the fridge, so he just stood there, dumbfounded.

Alice stood, gritting her teeth and grumbling under her breath. "All right, let's go," she ordered, her hand wrapped firmly around his, yanking him out of the kitchen.

ΔΔΔ

Kumo felt naked, standing awkwardly on the street corner in his black slacks and white button-up shirt. He missed his trench coat dreadfully. The wind, tunneling through the quiet streets, blew right through the thin cotton sweater *she* had forced him to wear. He shivered. *This is not improving my situation*, he thought. Alice enthusiastically flagged the nearest cab, maintaining her tight grip on the decidedly not-enthused Kumo. He'd already tried to escape her grasp several times, but to no avail. So he did his best to act as though he were alone. Soon they both were sitting in the back of a green taxi. Only once the cab began to move did Alice release Kumo's hand.

They rode in silence for a while before Kumo decided to say, "What made you think you could do that to my kitchen? And anyway, what were *you* still doing in *my* apartment? And another—"

"First of all, *you* invited *me* in! And secondly, I'll have you know, it's likely I saved your life today, Kuve!"

She expected him to disagree, and he would have if not for remembering her wise disposal of those long-dead "olives."

"And stop calling me *Kuve!* It's *Kumo!* Is that so hard?!"

"Now, now, Kuvey! That's no way to speak to a lady." She shoved her breasts out provocatively, which, though a cheap tactic, made for a highly effective way of winning the argument.

He groaned and stared out the window of his taxicab prison. When the streets began to look unfamiliar, he had to break his silence to ask, "So *where* exactly are we going?"

"We're going to dinner!"

Kumo's stomach growled at the words; he hadn't noticed how hungry he was. "What's wrong with *that* place?" he said, pointing out a random restaurant.

"Oh, heavens, no! Do you have *any* standards?"

"Well, yes, of course I do!" After speaking, Kumo immediately realized her question was rhetorical.

"You are hopeless, my dear. *Hopeless.*"

Kumo harumphed and turned away. "This place had better be *real* special." He didn't bother looking at Alice. He didn't expect a reply, and he didn't get one. Though had he been looking, he might have caught the brief sly grin that crept over her face.

The cab stopped in a dark alley beside a wide canal. A single street lamp buzzed with a sickly glow that cast strange shadows against the age-cracked pavement; fog creeped in from the canal behind them.

This was certainly not what Kumo had expected. He closed his eyes, hoping the cabbie was just stopping to check a map or something. But before he could take in his surroundings, Alice was standing outside.

"Come on, *Kuuuvey* dear! Time's a wastin'." Alice fluffed out her frilly skirt, stirring up the cloud of mist that had settled around her. She had gone shopping for them both while he had slept. She was still disappointed that she had had time to pick out only three outfits for each of them, but she had been in a bit of a hurry to be rid of her previous outfit and wasn't entirely certain when the boy would wake up.

"No way! Not a chance!" He couldn't think of a worse idea than getting out of the cab *here*. "Where the hell *are* we, anyway?"

"Come on! You of all people should know how to appreciate a little peace and quiet. Now, come on, scaredy-pants!"

Perhaps against his better judgment, Kumo pushed the taxi door open with his foot, got out, and made his way toward her with undisguised rage. He had planned on dragging her back into the cab, but before his hand could even reach her, the driver had already sped off into the darkness. He sighed and hung his head in silent defeat for some time before speaking again. "Lead on."

She pulled him into the dank alley. Kumo's mind raced as he blindly followed her. Why was he following her, anyway? Time had slowed in his mind as the world around him turned into a flurry of black and gray; the adrenaline that coursed through his veins made him both aware of and impartial to every subtle detail of his surroundings. The only thing that seemed real was the hand whose beautiful fingers wrapped gently around his. And in this moment of clarity, that hand captured his every sense in its delicate beauty.

For the first time, he allowed himself to notice *her*. So enraptured was he with really taking her in, he almost ran right into her back when she suddenly stopped. His eyes closed, and he braced for impact, but it never came.

He opened his eyes again to find himself standing right next to Alice, who didn't seem to have noticed anything out of the ordinary. "What was that about? Why did we stop—" As he spoke, Kumo realized that before them was a solid brick wall. "Well, *this* is certainly nice."

"Oh, shush! Don't be such a prat, or I won't take you next time." At that, she walked up to the wall and set her hand against it.

"Well, I sure would be disappointed to miss *this* in future. I—" Alice put a hand to the wall—and pushed into it, the bricks yielding to reveal a glowing display that filled the alleyway with an eerie blue light. She set her hand over the screen, and a clear beep sounded just before the bricks returned to normal.

"It's so good to be back," Alice sighed.

"What? And what in hell was *that?*"

Alice remained silent as she backed away slightly, standing completely still, and there was a flurry of pistons as a large segment of wall scraped inward. At first there was just smoke, but soon the alley was filled with a brilliantly bright light.

Alice turned to face Kumo, who watched in shock and awe, his feet heavy as anchors. "Welcome to my favorite little hole in the wall, dear. I dare say it is the best dining this side of the world has to offer." She smiled. "I guess that is awfully presumptuous of me to say, but if you want to have any hope of contradicting me, you'll have to try it."

And with that, her hand once again wrapped around his, and she dragged his enfeebled figure out of the dark alleyway and into the wall's crack of blinding light.

WALKING INTO "THE WALL"

Upon entering, Kumo noticed the lights suddenly dimmed, and the hall that moments before had seemed empty was filled by five silent sentinels, whose masked figures blocked the path ahead. He backed away in surprise, bumping into a guard who pushed him firmly to the place where he had previously stood.

I knew this girl was bad news. Kumo was certain he had just stepped into the middle of a Yakuza drug deal gone bad. Shaking, he longed for the safety of his home that now felt so distant.

Alice, however, stood calmly, bringing her hands upward and showing she had no weapons. She stared directly into the eyes of the masked man who seemed to be in charge. After a moment, he seemed satisfied and signaled to his men. Without delay, the menacing sentries silently parted, clearing the path as they returned to their posts. The lights returned, the watchers disappearing in the shadows that filled the halls.

Alice, suddenly realizing how frightened her companion was, broke the silence: "Oh! This club is rather ... *private*. Sorry I forgot to mention that tiny little detail."

Kumo's mind was numb; it was all just a little too much to take in. *What the hell kind of place is this?* He just hoped he wasn't getting caught up in something illegal, although when he thought about it, he was pretty sure he was. He almost expressed his fear to Alice, but the image of the strange masked men who had just disappeared flooded his mind, and he decided he had probably best not risk rubbing her, or them, the wrong way. *Just get through this, buddy. It'll be over soon.* Kumo often tried using different names when referring to himself in the third person. He had always hoped it would somehow help him to better cope with stressful situations, but either he was really-really stressed, or "buddy" wasn't going to make his short list of favorites.

Alice's hand reached out in a gesture she hoped would bring him some comfort. It felt odd touching his palms, not just because of how cold and clammy they were, but for the mere fact that she was holding someone else's hand in hers. The tingling sensation that shot across her every time she brushed against his ring did nothing to take away from how awkward she felt. Of course, while Kumo had little way of hiding his surprise, she was much more practiced in these affairs.

It was a few moments before his heart could recover not only from the unexpected encounter earlier, but also from the immediate rush that had overcome him as he experienced the softness of her touch. As far back as Kumo could remember, he had never known the tenderness others seemed to take for granted. He saw it all around him, but hard experience had taught him not to expect it for himself.

"You okay?"

He was dizzy, but he felt perhaps walking would ease the burden of the slow re-stitching of his mind. Eventually, however, he realized that a large part of his problem was that he had been holding his breath since well before she had reached out to touch him. He breathed deeply, but not *too* deeply, in an effort to be super casual-like about it. Of course, all this while feeling as though he had nearly drowned made that a little difficult.

They wound down several flights of stairs and passed many rooms that appeared occupied, which was confirmed by the occasional shouts of *"Banzai!"* that echoed from behind their doors.

"I can't wait to show you our room—it is positively delightful!" Alice squeezed Kumo's hand; there was a bounce in her step that increased in amplitude as they made their way farther down the hall of elegantly carved ebony doors. The long black bows of her lacy halter top swayed sexily as they went.

"Here we are!" Alice turned just in time to catch a glimpse of Kumo as his eyes wandered over her form. She smiled wryly, evidently enjoying the attention. She let go of his hand and did a slow little spin, making sure he had time to give her a good look. "You like it? I thought it was super cute, too!"

Kumo was blushing terribly by now, and it was a struggle to speak. "I-I'm sorry. I couldn't help it." He looked down as he spoke, shame welling up inside him.

"Now don't be silly! You don't think I dressed this well so you could just look at the ground, do you?" She grabbed both his hands and pulled herself close enough that her chest was directly in his line of sight. "Now pay a lovely lady the attention she deserves, or you risk making her feel all neglected and sad."

Kumo found himself holding his breath again as his wide-eyed head snapped to attention and he stared forward in barely hidden terror. Never mind his cheeks; his ears were bright red now too. Alice— who had been pouting rather convincingly—blew gently and whispered, "Breathe now, Kuvey dear," and as he finally breathed, she seemed once again satisfied, her former jovial expression returning in an instant.

"That's the spirit!" Alice smiled brightly and backed closer to the heavy-looking door, in the middle of which were carved three symbols that looked vaguely familiar to Kumo, but whose origins he couldn't quite place:

There was a low electrical hum, followed by three muted beeps. Kumo had just enough time to look around in confusion before his search was interrupted by the sudden sound of dozens of bolts crashing inward from the door. The door slid gently and freely into the adjacent wall as if of its own volition.

What greeted Kumo was strange beyond anything he had experienced so far. Over the room's threshold the floor changed from tile to calf-high Bermuda grass. The sound of frogs and flowing water filled the air. He watched glow bugs glide from one sweet-smelling patch of lemon grass to another. A cool breeze carrying a thousand different scents emanated from the room, beckoning him to enter.

Kumo stepped softly onto mud and grass. He lost his balance for a moment, and he would have fallen if his hand wasn't wrapped in Alice's warm grip. It had bothered him at first, but there was now an unfamiliar comfort in the gentle way her fingers enclosed his.

The door shut behind them, and it was as if they had just stepped outside, until he noticed that the starry sky was filled with several large and unfamiliar bodies that burned slowly over not-quite-recognizable constellations. Something was amiss.

"What is this? Where are we?"

"This, my dear, is my little piece of 'The Wall.'" She let go of one of his hands to make a wide sweeping gesture covering the entire expanse as she spoke. "I'll tell you what—it cost me a pretty penny, too! 'It can't be done, Miss,' they said! But, as you can see, a little money goes a long way toward changing things in these parts."

"Clearly ..."

"Follow me. It gets better!"

Kumo watched as she flitted into the darkness. He turned to look back at the door, but all that greeted him was a wall of stone. He sighed and turned to follow her, grumbling under his breath as his boots sloshed obnoxiously in the mud.

He followed the dark path that led through the woods as quickly as he could, the forest blotting out the moonlit sky, making it increasingly difficult to navigate. He stopped for a moment, listening to the hooting of owls that roosted above him in the otherwise spooky quiet of that particular patch of forest.

"Come on, Kuuvey!"

Kumo jumped and shrieked simultaneously. "Don't creep up on me like that!"

Alice giggled. "Oh ... did I scare you?"

After a moment, he lied: "No." He wasn't very convincing.

"Well then, what's the problem?"

"Nothing. Let's go." Kumo strutted forward, not knowing where he was going, until Alice's hand grabbed his shoulder.

"No more detours," she said gently. "I'm getting hungry." This time Alice walked slowly next to him as they went. It was not long before they reached a clearing in the woods. They came upon a table carved expertly from the trunk of a tree that once must have stood proudly in the center of the glade, the place to which its roots still desperately clung. The flickering red light of two large candles coalesced with the blue glow that coursed down from the heavens, revealing two crystal glasses that lay in wait.

Kumo and Alice sat across from each other in two chairs that were carved from dark-stained wood.

"So ... now what?" Kumo looked around in expectation, the fear creeping back up on him a bit.

"Now, we order," she said. She pushed the red leather menu toward him; he took it skeptically.

"What exactly am I supposed to do with this?" he said, quickly scanning the menu. "Wanting the miso soup and the char-grilled chicken soba isn't going to make it magically appear."

"Now, don't be rude, Kumo." She snapped her fingers. Only moments had passed before a masked figure came forth from the shadows and waited silently next to her. "We order."

Kumo, who was really getting tired of all the surprises, stared at Alice incredulously, unable to produce anything more than a stammer.

"He will have the char-grilled chicken soba and miso soup. I will have my usual."

Kumo remained silent until the waiter had disappeared into the shadows, at which point he let out a heavy sigh. Only when he took a breath did he realize that, once again, he had been holding it the whole time. Which made him briefly consider whether he perhaps had a problem with the whole breathing thing in the first place.

"Don't take them so seriously! Relax. Enjoy yourself for once."

"Sorry."

"Now ... tell me about yourself." As she spoke, Alice poured wine from a bottle Kumo had failed to notice the waiter had left behind.

"Me? Umm ... there's not much to tell."

"Nonsense! A man who knows of Masoudi deserves more credit than that." She stared expectantly into his eyes, holding out a glass of red wine. Reluctantly, Kumo took it.

"I don't know ... What do you want to know?" Unable to match her gaze, he stared at the wine, swirling it nervously as he looked around him in hopes of some means to dampen the blow that would surely come when he braved a taste.

This was a game Alice enjoyed, and it showed. "First of all, while we are on the topic, how did you come to read Masoudi's work?"

"I am an archeologist ... Well, I am still finishing up, *technically*, but I have been working on some Islamic artifacts, and I have found a little research often goes a long way to explain anomalies."

"See! You *are* interesting. *Very interesting*." She inched closer, plopping her chin in her hands as she spoke. "So, Mister Archeologist ... anything else?"

"Well, I currently do security for a library." Though Alice had already nearly emptied her glass, Kumo had just decided to brave his first sip when he finished speaking. He had hoped he would be able to impress her, but even though he knew it was coming, his face still twisted in revulsion at the bitter aftertaste.

Alice giggled. "Not your *toxin of choice*, I gather?"

"N-No … not really," he said, choking a little on his words as he attempted to get the taste off his tongue by scraping it with his front teeth.

The waiter slunk in from the darkness, and before any more could be said, he had vanished, leaving two hot silver platters that steamed wildly as their lids were lifted.

Kumo drank his miso soup hastily, grateful for any change in taste. Only once his bowl was empty did he look up to see her smiling face.

"Good?"

He grunted contentedly as he swallowed the last of the chicken soba and washed it down with the few remaining drops of miso soup. He noticed that she had only just touched her own food, and he would have felt ashamed were it not for the joy of that last wave of flavor.

"Delicious. Thank you." He had almost forgotten the wine … but just almost.

"Anytime, dear. Now, what did you mean by 'security'?" she said, poking at her salad with a fork.

"Oh, I just work for the Diet."

"That sounds kinda cool," she lied.

"Not really. Nobody actually bothers the library. Mostly we keep out ghosts, really."

"Wow ... ghosts, you say?" That was more interesting sounding.

Kumo shook his head, rolling his eyes. "Umm, no ... That was a joke. We just watch the place. In fact, I don't know if anyone has ever even tried anything, but I kinda get a private library out of the deal."

"Well, even *I* can't make that claim," she lied again.

This was it; he couldn't bear it a moment longer. Kumo took a deep breath. "Alice?"

"Yes?"

"Doesn't it bother you?" He pointed to himself.

"What? That piece of soba hanging off your chin?" She pointed at the noodle.

He wiped his face embarrassedly, "No, I mean, how I am. Doesn't it bother you?" He strained against the desire to simply run away. Though he feared ruining the experience, he could no longer resist the urge to believe that she was *really* sitting there with him. It was an apparent reality from which recovery would grow increasingly difficult the longer he stayed.

"Oh ... *that?*" She pushed her hands across the table next to his, looking back and forth between the two as though it were the first time she had noticed the difference. "Nope. Doesn't bother me, though I guess it was worth checking." Her face was very serious. There was a long pause as they stared into each other's eyes.

Suddenly, the awkward silence was broken; both burst into laughter, shattering the tension that had hung in the air like an overfilled balloon. As he brayed uncontrollably, Kumo was filled with such relief as he had never felt before, despite his inability to contain himself. Alice, too, felt some relief as she giggled and sniggered a little.

She held her breath, pursing her lips shut, her eyes bugging out just a little as she continued to chortle. Despite the effort it took, she managed to take his hand in hers and stand.

"Come"—*snort*—"with me."

Kumo, unable to summon the control she had shown in speaking, simply complied.

It wasn't long before the guffaws no longer echoed through the woods as the two walked quietly, hand in hand.

Eventually, they came upon the stream's shore, very near to which lay a small waterfall serenely lit by the patches of luminous moss that lined its rocky bottom. Without a word, the two sat in a particularly comfortable patch of grass. Content to lie silently beside each other, they watched the stars' warped reflections leaping from the columns of water that plummeted to the frothy pool below. They lay sprawled out for some time before Kumo broke the silence.

"How does it work?"

"Hmm?"

"The sky ... how does it work?" His mouth felt particularly dry as he spoke, and he thought, perhaps ... but no, the air was as moist as it had ever been.

"Oh, wanna see?" Alison quickly produced a small silver remote from her brassiere. She delicately turned a knob. At first, Kumo noticed nothing, but soon he saw that the stars above were streaking across the sky at an unusual—no, a frantic—pace. It was only moments later that the sun had peeked its head over the tree line, bringing a sudden silence to the forest as each creature in it looked up. And then it was midday, and another sun joined the sky quite unexpectedly.

Kumo felt dizzy as he watched it all, his stomach turning as the clouds quickened their pace coming in and out of existence, drifting here and there, going as it would seem where e'er they fancied to be. In moments, several moons rose over the horizon, and the sky was once again filled with thousands of shimmering stars that raced by dizzyingly. There were a few last dazed chirps from the birds that had only just begun to sing, and then there was silence but for the sound of Alice and Kumo's breath as the sky slowed to a more natural pace.

"To answer your question, dear ... screens ... lights and screens ... thousands of them," Alice whispered quietly as she lay staring into the sky.

"Genius ... simply genius, but, my god, how much did this cost!?"

"I am glad you like it." She ignored his question, because it was rude.

Kumo didn't feel the need to press the issue. He felt very tired, his arms heavy as he stretched them out above his head. They lay there next to each other for what seemed to him hours, talking about all kinds of things, the details of which were not relayed to me—you see, the account I received got rather fuzzy at about this point. What was clear, however, was that he remembered lying contently as they listened to the many sounds of the strange world around them, peering ever upward into the simulated expanse of stars and galaxies, following their graceful ebb and flow as they drifted by.

SIREN'S SNARE

She did not know how it had happened, but she was doing it again. She was, in spite of herself, watching him sleep for a second time, listening to the soft circulation of his snores, observing the rippling of his white buttoned top as the wind rushed over him.

"No! It is not right—not part of the plan!" It was with some difficulty that she ripped her gaze from him. "Why now? Why *him?*" she thought, and though she was silent, there was an ear-piercing scream from inside her.

All these years of planning, all of the pain you have known in the search! How dare you think of giving up, now when you are so close?

"But, I ... I don't know ... how can I believe that it is even still there? How can I hope to find a way?"

You are weak! Unworthy and weak! How dare you even think it? Of course, there is yet hope. Why now, of all times, do you choose to be so ... so human?!

Her eyes were shut tightly as the war raged on inside her. She clutched at her chest in anguish, unable even to glance in the direction of her companion for fear of the consequences. She could barely remember the last time someone had made her heart skip a beat, and yet, annoyingly, this awkward excuse for a boy did just that.

It was, after all, you who set this plan into motion, was it not?

"Yes, bu—"

And was it not you who even went so far as to slip a pinch of sedative into his cup, making light work lighter still?

She had no response for that.

All these things she could not deny she had done, but now that she faced her quarry head-on, she suddenly found herself trying to reason out another way. "But, what if we took him with us? Perhaps he would give it freely."

Just take it! It is folly to linger now; be done with this foolish attempt at distraction! She felt her arm edging outward though she willed it not to.

"No! I won't! There must be another way!" But try though she might to stop it, it was already done.

There is not. What has come over you, girl?

"NO! STOP! PUT IT BACK!" She felt it, felt as her fingers pried it from his, felt as the ring dropped heavily into her palm, an angry sting against her flesh. Then, in an instant, she was gone, a shadow amongst shadows as she sprinted through the night. And though she ran, she could not flee from her tears nor escape her misery.

ΔΔΔ

It was to a nasty headache and the sound of nearby pecking that Kumo awoke. A group of kiwis foraging near his head, pulling a long worm from the ground, squabbled excitedly as they ripped it apart, distributing it, if only by accident, into relatively even portions that wriggled madly as they were swallowed.

Kumo noticed all around him the chirping of many birds and the smell of exotic tropical plants. The familiar rustle of lemon grass now mingled with the calming trill of the speckle-chested piculet. When at last he opened his eyes, he was greeted by a bright sky, blue dotted by white clouds. All these things, though he did enjoy them, did nothing to alleviate the pain that throbbed through his skull. Since he had never been drugged before, however, this explanation for his hang-over did not occur to him at the time.

He groaned, his hand searching for Alice's as he watched a pair of piculets spin mirthfully about, slowly circling each other. Then, he reached with the other, but still nothing. Only upon sitting up did he realize how terribly sore he was. *Guess that's what I get for sleeping on a lump of grass in the middle of the woods.*

"Alice?"

After a short struggle, he was on his feet, stretching painfully. *Where could she have run off to?* It was then, as his gaze traveled to the falls, that he saw ... *the sentinel.*

The masked figure crouched with unnerving stillness, perched on a boulder in the middle of the pool, just in front of the waterfall. He looked almost as though he were meditating, but while letting his heavily armored arms hang limply at his sides. For the first time, Kumo could see clearly what his guard's armor was made of: a mix of bronze and aged, patina-green copper which, despite being muted by a dark lacquer, shone brightly in the midday sun.

The figure, too, had noticed Kumo. It sprang lightly into the air, landing with an unexpected ease, gracefully traversing the sparsely laid stones that jutted out from the rippling water. If there had been a sound—the apparent weight of the armor it donned notwithstanding—it was barely detectable.

Not knowing what to do, Kumo stood perfectly still, unsure of his welcome here without the presence of his trusted guide.

"Kuve." It was the first time Kumo had heard one speak. The voice was gruff and echoed deeply from within the solid helmet. This was a *he*, judging by the voice buried somewhere inside it.

"Kumo, actually …" Surprisingly, he was able to speak as well, though it did not come easily.

"Petty difference it makes. Lady Ael—Alison— had urgent matters to attend to. She has asked that

I convey her deepest apologies." His tone was indifferent at best, and the angry face whose terrifying features lay forged in metal, cold and motionless before him, did little to put him in a state of ease. "Come. I shall be your escort from this place."

The bewildered Kumo was almost immediately herded across the unfamiliar forest floor.

"This is a nice place you all have here."

Silence from the figure.

"So many varieties of plants and animals! It must have taken ages." Kumo nearly tripped over an exposed root as he spoke. The sentinel grumbled at the time it took Kumo to regain his balance. "So … how long did this take? To put all of *this* together?"

"That is of little consequence to you." Kumo correctly interpreted this less-than-subtle hint from the sentinel that it might be a good time for him to shut up.

They trod along for some time in an awkward silence, until Kumo could no longer contain himself. "How did you get that armor? It looks very old." He was intrigued by the craftsmanship and the perfect condition of the armor his sentry wore.

"I am no jester, you fool. Learn to still the wag of that tongue, lest I take it from you. Lady Alison gave no mention of you keeping it."

Kumo did not doubt the sentinel would make good on his threat as his eyes fixed on the hand that was now set firmly at the hilt of a katana, a katana whose black sheath glinted in the light that slipped in through the leafy canopy above. Kumo found himself quite suddenly and violently ripped from the clouds where he had blissfully floated since the night before, back down to the cold reality in which he had no idea where exactly he was or why he found himself in the presence of such ill-tempered company. He was very careful, from that point forward, to ponder in silence, not wishing to further test the last length of fuse in the most unpleasant usher he'd ever had the *wonderfully* good fortune of meeting.

Alison's piece of "The Wall" seemed a very different place under the perfect imitation of daylight. He could see bright reflections of fishes' scales under the surface of the stream next to which they marched. In fact, there were dozens of strange and rare varieties of flora and fauna in every direction he looked. He would probably have enjoyed his surroundings more were it not for the angry figure that shoved him forcibly from behind whenever Kumo showed any sign of dawdling because something had caught his interest.

Eventually they came upon a dead end, a stone wall that seemed to stretch upward into infinity, though he was certain it was at least in part an illusion.

"Stand back."

Kumo, not wishing to invite any more threats, did as he was told and watched as the door appeared and opened. It happened much in the same manner as it had in the alleyway the night before, except that this time what was revealed was the familiar hallway from which he had earlier come.

Soon, they had reached the same small dark entryway in which they had first encountered each other, and Kumo had all but slipped out into the world when he was stopped mid stride by his guide's heavily armored gauntlet.

"Lady Alison asked that I give you this. A parting gift." A silver pendant was thrust into his hands.

When Kumo looked up from the pendant, he found the sentinel and doorway had vanished, as though it had all been a dream.

The pendant was gold and silver and felt scaly in his hand. Upon further inspection, Kumo could see that it was an intricately crafted likeness of two dragons: one silver and the other gold, with each dragon devouring the other's tail and wrapped around each other to form the symbol of infinity.

It almost looked like one of the dragons had a bird's beak, and the other was some sort of viper. He couldn't remember anything in his studies like it, but it struck him as oddly familiar.

He studied it as he walked, wondering what business could be so important that Alice had left him in the night. Surprisingly, despite her abrupt departure and leaving him in the care of the inhospitable guard, he still earnestly hoped he would see her again soon.

Behind the dragons lay a simple silver tag, upon which were etched the same three symbols that were carved on the door to Alice's sanctuary. The pendant hung from a chain made of thousands of tiny rings, each so small they were almost invisible to the naked eye as they wove together forming the chain itself. Its workmanship was unmatched by anything he had ever seen.

As Kumo ambled out onto the cracked pavement, he found that he felt much less foreboding than the night before. Still, as he pulled his phone from his pocket, he turned over the memory of the less-than-friendly farewell he had received and decided it would be some time before another visit to "The Wall" was in order.

To Kumo's dismay, he found himself smack dab in the middle of the Sashima district, at least an hour's walk from the nearest train station in Minami-ku. These were places with which he was unfamiliar; he gathered that he was just outside Tokyo, but that was the only sense of things that he had. He pulled out his wallet, counting the diminutive stack of bills he pulled from inside. Finding his wallet no richer than it had been the night before, he gave up on the hope of being able to afford a cab without his cards and began the drudgery of what he expected would be a long, long journey home.

THE DIP

The day was still young, something Kumo was not accustomed to experiencing consciously. He looked up over the calm waters of what he now knew to be the Tonegawa River and noticed a patch of particularly angry-looking gray nimbus clouds on the horizon.

That's exactly what I need ... rain. He quickened his pace, not expecting any favors from the heavens but hoping he could make the station before the bad weather arrived. Normally, Kumo would have been rather pleased by the storm's imminent approach; after all, rain tended to drive most people indoors. Today, however, he was facing a four-hour journey—a good part of which had to be made on foot. Being wet would add considerably to his discomfort.

He scurried onward, glad for the fresh insoles in his boots. But, comfortable though they were, they couldn't get him to the station before the downpour hit.

∆∆∆

The loud squishing of boots heralded the man's arrival at the Minami-ku station, and, whether he knew it or not, he was being watched as he slogged his way through one more rain-soaked street before slumping on the nearest covered bench.

Interesting. The boy was fascinated by the man's strange likeness to an undead creature—this intrigued him entirely too much, he admitted, but that acknowledgment did nothing to diminish his curiosity.

The boy stood no taller than four feet high and was careful to blend in with the small crowds of passengers who, to his dismay, gave the man—at least in his opinion—a wider berth than necessary. The man's silver-white hair was completely drenched and hung in clumps over his eyes. Further scrutiny revealed that the man was agitated, cursing under his breath. Clearly, the man was distracted. *That should play to my advantage, at least!* the boy thought.

Now, this boy was no amateur; he knew that this man would make a terrible mark (the crowds were leaving too much space around the man), but his mind was already made up. He was going to get a closer look at him and at whatever else he could manage, like, say, the contents of the man's pockets.

The man rung out his hair, and it was as if a flood had been unleashed—it was surprising how much water there was. The boy kept expecting him to be done, but by the time he had finished, the train was nearly upon them. He followed as the man rose with a low groan from his spot and wandered over to take a place behind the white line.

As he gathered information, the boy was trying his best to come to a solid plan. He could work within the tight spaces of the train, but getting close enough without drawing attention was still going to be a challenge.

To his relief, however, the moment they were on the train, two things changed. First, the man visibly calmed down. Granted, this in itself would not have necessarily made the boy happy, but it seemed to be facilitating the second change—the formerly aloof crowds appeared willing to overlook the man's oddness in exchange for whatever legroom they could secure. Glee spread from his toes up when the boy noticed how the object of his pursuit sagged in his seat. The poor man must be terribly, terribly tired.

Perhaps not so bad a mark after all!

The boy waited and watched; he could almost feel *the* moment coming. His brother had told him what it felt like just before the big heist, and he imagined it feeling something like this. "The heightened sense of things, you know" is how he explained it.

Finally, the moment he had been waiting for had come. Those frightening bloodred eyes that had been drooping since the train left the station finally closed. The sopping mess of a man had dozed off.

Perfect! The boy bided his time just long enough to be sure of his success, checking the distance to the next stop. *Only seconds to go!* The boy had seen where the man kept his wallet when he had produced his pass to enter the station, so he knew where his prize lay.

Ha! Take that! With impeccable execution, the gaunt black wallet made the transition from the man's pocket into his own in less than the blink of an eye. His smile broadened as he soaked up the glory of it all—a train packed near to overflowing and not a soul had noticed that flawless demonstration of his skills.

He beamed, making to stroll casually from the scene, when by some unfortunate chance, the train's wheels squealed, and the train came to a sudden halt. Quite contrary to the boy's plans, he found himself peering into those scarlet windows just as they fluttered open. Whatever was written on the thief's face, it gave him away as up to no good. The man stared at the boy; the boy stared at the man. Neither moved, each seemingly locked in place.

Then, the man reached his hand down, patting his pocket. His suspicions were confirmed; the chase was on! Before he could grasp the ruffian, however, the boy was already out the door. In seconds, the pickpocket was at a full sprint, knowing—as luck would have it—exactly where he was going.

The boy slipped easily through the crowds, darting in and out of view as Kumo skirted between the protective bubbles that most like to keep for themselves in public places. Though his progress wasn't much slower, it was certainly less graceful as he rammed through the masses of people who probably hadn't even noticed the child he was chasing.

Behind him, the boy heard the sound of objects flying from hands, followed by angry cries; he heard the man's gallant command of "Stop! Thief!" None of this worried him so much as the fact that, as he heard these things, their source seemed to be growing ever closer.

He turned his head only once, but the sight of the beast of a man that raged behind him was more than enough encouragement to quicken his step to a pace he had never attempted to reach before. Not much later he found himself crouched behind a dumpster in an alleyway, hurriedly ripping the accursed prize from his pocket. He opened it, quickly taking note of the lack of any credit cards or, well, just about anything, really.

You've gotta be kiddin' me! A mere twelve yen was all that greeted him. *Twelve yen!* There may as well have just been blank paper inside; at least that he would have had some hope of using. He was positively fuming, but there was no time for further delay. Much to his chagrin, the man had most inconveniently found his hiding place. The boy made no effort to hide his contempt as he stuffed the paltry sum into his pocket, tossing the wallet at his mark's feet.

The wallet skidded lamely, bouncing once off a rotten apple before thudding against the man's wet black leather boots. To the boy's relief, the man stopped, taking the wallet in his hand and looking it over. All the while, the boy backed up cautiously, step by step by creeping step, each one taking him that much farther toward freedom.

Relief was just beginning to fill him, and he was almost ready to turn and run when it happened: something caught the man's eye, something the boy did not see. Suddenly, there was a rage the likes of which this young lad had never seen before. Sure, he had witnessed greed, hatred, and a great number of unpleasant things, but this was different— the rage filling the man's expression seemed almost … unnatural.

All this for twelve yen!? You gotta be kidding me!

The boy's eyes were wide as he turned tail and fled. He heard the vicious growl behind him, and the spattering gallop that followed, but he dared not look back. In a last-ditch effort to dissuade his pursuer, he flung the tiny handful of yen into the air. They gently fluttered to the ground unnoticed by the madman as he whizzed past.

The boy was running, running, running! That was all he could dedicate his mind to; he wasn't even sure if he was breathing anymore. All he knew was that one foot kept leaping in front of the other, carrying him god knows where. Anywhere but there, anywhere safe from—but it was too late. He was caught in the pale pursuer's snare.

This's it! I'm done for!

His captor raised him up off the ground, holding fast to the red coat collar that no longer hung loosely at his nape. Though he kicked and shouted angrily, the little ruffian was powerless to do anything but hang helplessly in the air.

"The ring ... hand it over." The words came slowly through clenched teeth as every syllable was enunciated with force. The boy thought he could practically taste the menace on the man's breath as he spoke (though it was likely just old nasty soba).

The boy whipped his head frantically about, searching for something, anything, that could save him, and then he saw them—his "family" had come to the rescue. It had to be them.

"You'll pay for this, mister!" The little man crossed his arms defiantly, a wide smirk across his face in spite of the fact that he was hanging in the air by his coat collar.

Perhaps had he caught sight of the expressions his family wore, he wouldn't have been so sure of himself.

ΔΔΔ

Kumo's hands shook in anger; his eyes twitched as he stared at the boy's haughty little face. He wanted nothing more than to extinguish it from existence. A dreadful pain throbbed where his ring had once been. The pain only increased his rage.

"Giv—" *Who was that approaching?*

But, it was too late. The last thing Kumo saw were two heavy arms dropping a burlap sack over his head. He felt the squirming hoodlum being taken from his grasp. Then, with a loud crack, Kumo's world become nothing but shocking pain.

SEETHING

Meanwhile, the storm that had drenched Kumo at the Minami-ku station had swept slowly over Suita and washed out all the gutters in Osaka. Not long after ruining the polish on the shoes of various businessmen, the storm continued its journey and was joined by another group of gray clouds that had been making a right mess of things over the Yodo River for some time. Together, the storms meandered down the river until they dumped out over Osaka Bay and passed through the Kiisuido Strait, gathering fury and strength all the way.

There, in the ocean, floated the smooth bright bow of *The Stranded One*. Her stainless-steel hull was so reflective that the vessel almost blended into the swells that now rose higher and higher as the winds picked up and the sky darkened overhead. Above deck, there was a bustle of crewmen battening down the hatches and checking the straps on anything that might get knocked loose in the coming storm. Below decks, through one of the nine portholes that lined the ship's lowest levels, Alice sat cross-legged on the bed of an elegantly decorated stateroom. She peered enthusiastically at something small and shiny that lay in her palm.

"Now, let us examine our prize," she spoke in English as she shifted the golden ring around in the flickering light, the ring for which so many long years had been spent in desperate search.

"A proud day." There was almost a twinge of remorse in her words, but she managed to stifle it.

Indeed. This day has been long in the making. The deep voice felt calmer than usual, almost reassuring.

"Yes ... Yes, it has." With a measure of relief, she examined the perfect sphere of amber-colored material that crested the interwoven strands of gold and platinum that made up the ring's band. This was what she had sought all along, but the victory felt unexpectedly hollow now.

"Why couldn't we hav—"

Why, indeed! The reassurance in the voice was gone in an instant, replaced by the more familiar impatient rage.

"It-It's nothing."

Nothing is nothing. That was most definitely not nothing back there! he snarled.

"It is not important now!" Though she doubted her words, she hoped they would be enough to appease him.

On that point we can agree! Now open it and be done with this fool's errand!

Alice ran her fingernail along the creases beneath the glimmering stone, searching. Moments later, she found it; inside, a tiny latch clicked, and the ring that had seemed before to be a solid mass of metal and amber opened to reveal a tiny compartment.

"Now let's s—" her stomach lurched as she was instantly filled with terrible horror at what she saw— or, rather, at what she did not see. What greeted her eyes was ... nothing; the compartment was completely and thoroughly empty.

What is this?!

"It cannot have ..."

Oh! It cannot, you say. But it has, you fool!

She stared in disbelief as a tiny beam of light shone through a hole in the compartment door as she held it up to inspect it closer. The hole was so small that it hadn't been visible before she opened the compartment.

Only you would be so foolish as not to notice this!

"I-I ... This is your fault!"

My fault? My fault! How dare you even think it! This whole mess is your doing! If it were not for you-

"If it were not for me, you would not even exist now!"

His growl filled her mind, but he said nothing for the moment.

She angrily snapped the compartment shut, wrapping her palm in a fist around the band. Her knuckles were white from the force they exerted on the ring as she squeezed. She closed her eyes, taking a deep breath of the cool salty ocean air. A smile crept over her face. "This time ... This time, we do things my way."

Oh, your way, you say? And what would that be? Shall we go drink ourselves into oblivion again?

117

Or would you prefer to sate one of your many other less endearing vices?

"Shut up! I am calling the shots from now on."

Believe whatever you like. It changes nothing!

Alice was feeling oddly cheery, all things considered; there was a certain joy to be had in his failure ... even if it was her own failure as well.

She tore the terrifying mask from the countertop next to which she now stood, fastening it over her face as she donned a fine black-plated cataphract.

She passed no one as she made her way to the upper deck; it was some time before she came to a stop before the masked man who earlier had served as an escort to Kumo. He stood at the vessel's helm, overseeing the preparations for the storm.

"My Ladyship." His voice was different from earlier, though not by much. There was, however, an unmistakable reverence to his tone now, as he stood in her presence. "How may I be of service?"

"We return to port, Göttrick. I've some unfinished business to attend to."

BURIED

When Kumo finally awoke some time later, it was to a muffled scream in the distance and a throbbing pain that shot down from the top of his skull through each of his limbs as he tried to move. His world was darkness, and he could smell old blood on the burlap sack that scratched against his face as he struggled against the shackles that held his arms uncomfortably high above his head. Struggle though he did against his bindings, there was nothing to be done. He was trapped there in the darkness ... wherever *there* was.

He would have continued to struggle, but suddenly a shiver went down his spine as another scream echoed into his cell through the wall behind him. He pressed his burlap-covered ear to the cold stone wall and listened.

"How dare you lead him here, you fool!" A gruff voice boomed with anger.

"I-I-I di-didn't know!" This voice was shrill, familiar, and sounded more than a little frightened.

Kumo heard something slamming into the wall behind him as another scream rang out.

"DID NOT KNOW!?" A hard *slap* resounded through the darkness. "YOU INSOLENT FOOL! LOOK AT THE MARKS ON THIS PENDANT HE WAS WEARING, BOY!"

Kumo could barely hear the boy's wheezing breath. "I-I don't understand ... it's broke in half, anyways" was his barely audible response after some delay. "What is it?"

"It is death, you fool, and you have brought it straight to us." The man's voice was still angry, though quieter now.

"How was I supposed to know?"

"SILENCE!" There was another loud crash, possibly in response to the hint of indignation in the boy's voice. "Give me the ring, and we just might let you live."

Kumo could hear sobs between labored breaths. "Wh-what ... ring ...?"

"Don't play dumb with me, you nitwit. We heard him demanding his ring, and there wasn't anyone else around to have taken it."

"My brother'll kill you if you don't lemme go!"

The boy's assailant laughed. "Your brother can't save you from this place. He doesn't even know it exists. The ring is your only way out of here, so just tell me where you stowed it."

The boy whimpered in confusion. "I didn't take nothin' … I swear! Please … just let me go, mister!"

The man's cackle led Kumo to imagine he was smirking at his captive's panic. "Your lack of cooperation is … unfortunate for you. Maybe what you need is some convincing, boy. And as luck would have it, I happen to be something of an expert at convincing." As the man spoke, Kumo could make out the sound of metal knocking against metal. "You might say it is one of my gifts, actually."

"No! Please, sir, I swear I never saw a ring!" the boy choked out before his screams again filled the air, his pleas ignored. This time his wails were prolonged—and accompanied by a sizzling sound almost like that of bacon in a frying pan.

The boy kept repeating "I don't have it!" amidst his desperate shrieks, but clearly his captor was still not satisfied that this information was the truth. The man no longer spoke, but the sizzling and screams repeated for some time, until finally the boy too became silent.

"This is going to take longer than I thought," the angry man griped. Kumo heard a dragging sound and then a heavy-sounding door creaked open.

Kumo counted every step. Closer and closer grew the sounds of heavy footsteps that slowly overshadowed the sound of the boy's labored breathing. Closer. Still closer. Then, the door to Kumo's cell scraped open, and a cold draft of stale air rushed in and wrapped around him. Kumo's heart pounded furiously, and all he wanted was to run, but he felt like he couldn't even breathe as the dreaded footsteps approached him. He gasped in fear as uncomfortably hot breath poured through the sack that covered his head.

He heard a click, and his wrists were released from the shackles above him. For a moment, his bare feet finally touched the cold, coarse floor, and he tried to decide what to do. Before any choice could be made, however, two hands seized his thin, frail wrists with brutal strength.

Kumo struggled helplessly to right himself as his body dragged painfully across the rough stone floor. "Let me go!" he screamed in anger.

His captor chuckled as he gave Kumo's wrists a sharp jerk and yanked Kumo across the ground more forcefully than he had before. Just as Kumo was sure that the painful journey would never end, he found himself pitched into a hard and sturdy wooden chair. He felt himself strapped tightly, limb by limb, into its slick and cold embrace.

"Now, then ..." The burlap sack was ripped from Kumo's head. The face of a burly and scar-ridden man lay inches from his own, the smell of death wafting from the man's crusty lips as he spoke. "What are we going to do about you?"

A FLASH IN THE NIGHT

Far away, the cold night's sky lay dark and ominous above the western edge of Bristol. The looming clouds, forming an almost living veil, concealed the stars and shrouded the moonless heavens in mystery. This murkiness above might have caused one to wonder if some wrathful deity had not plucked the stars from their places of honor, for not one could be seen shining down upon the world's inhabitants. Instead, there were only the many artificial bright lights that lined the whole of Clifton Bridge, doing all they could to proclaim their own fictitious glory. Their attempts at resplendence and grandeur, however, were but a poor imitation of Nature's riches.

The young traveler did not take notice of the bridge's lights, or of much of anything else of his surroundings. Instead, he passed through the tall stone pillars that arched upward into each other, taking the shape of a large "A" that towered over Gloucester Road—an all-but-empty thoroughfare of little consequence, except that he had chosen it as his way.

Gauging by how tired he felt, it was probably several hours past midnight, but that mattered little to him then. His feet had only just left the bridge behind them, and he had no intention of stopping now. Not now that he had nowhere else left to go. Once he passed the bright lights of the bridge, it was not long before they were barely a glow in the distance.

Just then, breaking the street's solitude, an old and underloved Cooper sped recklessly by. Flying from its window came a piece of rubbish that glinted briefly from the darkness. Before it could touch the ground, the refuse was engulfed in a flurry of brilliant emerald-green flames—flames that hovered almost defiantly, as if to mock gravity. Beside this strange emerald light that pierced the night was the silhouette of the young man. He stood there with one palm outstretched in the direction of the flames, while his other hand clutched at something that lay beneath his shirt, upon his chest.

This odd scene held for an instant, then his palm closed, and the rich green blaze vanished, leaving the overgrown patch of Leigh Woods once again devoid of light.

"Litter bugs ..." he growled under his breath.

The man was surprised by how good it felt, how different it was now with its aid, and he hated himself for that small part of him that was briefly glad for what had come to pass. It is unknown whether he decided anything as he stood there in silence, counting the reasons he hated the world's cruel ways. What is certain, however, is that when he resumed his journey, he found himself changing his course; it was not long before the dark forest had him in its unwelcoming embrace.

The cobweb-ridden branches crashed painfully into his face, but he did not care how much it hurt. The many vines that filled the forest wrapped willfully around him in their pestiferous attempts at dissuasion, but he marched ahead, unhampered by their efforts.

He stormed ever onward, unfazed by the overgrown world that did not want him, until, by snap of branch and rip of vine, he found himself standing wholly surrounded and utterly alone at the forest's heart. It was only then, as he came to a sudden stop, fists clenched and knees shaking, that he found himself overcome.

Upon his knees he fell, and there he stayed, his hands upon his chest, as he peered up into the great nothingness above.

"WHY?!" was his cry to the heavens as the tears he had fought with such desperation let loose in a furious cascade, an outpouring that seemed only to leave him feeling emptier than ever.

There, finally acknowledging, expressing, the wretchedness caused by his loss, he murmured sounds of madness and despair into the cold uncaring world around him. Not more than a second passed when a blinding pillar of light, brilliant blue and white in hue, engulfed him, shooting straight up from the ground into the sky as far as the eye could see.

"Why?!" he repeated again and again, each time the pillar growing in brightness and girth until much of the wood was filled with its brilliance. Bolts of lightning shot from his mouth and eyes, leaving the atmosphere charged and pushing him to his limits. But, no matter how far his light was cast, no matter how loud the crack of lightning resounded or how desperately his cries echoed over the land, he knew no answer would come.

Thus, letting go of his chest, he allowed himself once more to be plunged into darkness, where he fell upon the ground and did not stir.

RECOVERING THE PRIZE

Alice stood in the alley behind the dumpster where Kumo had last been seen; the smell that filled the air was a toxic mix of motor oil and rotting food from the restaurant that stood on the building's other side. It had been three days since she had left him in the night, and there hadn't been a moment of peace from the regret that was only made worse by the voice that constantly reminded her of her failure.

You had it in your grasp, and what did you do? You let it go, you fool! Alice cringed as his voice berated her once again.

"I know! I know! Just let me concentrate for once!" She hadn't had a drink in three and a half days, which meant that the voice was louder than ever. All she wanted—all she ever wanted anymore——was a moment of quiet, but, alas, it never came.

Well, excuse me, missy, but leaving you to your own devices hasn't exactly gotten us anywhere thus far, has it?

"Oh, and your solution worked out sooooo much better, did it?!"

When did you get so sentimental, anyway? You seemed so desperate to find it before.

It was true she had spent many long years searching for the ring. As it seems with most things, it was only as she finally began to lose hope of finding it that it finally made its presence known.

"What is the point, anyway? He ... He is long gone by now; what is there left to return to?" Even she could not keep a single tear from forming as she dared to utter the words.

You would dare to abandon me?! The mockery in the voice had been replaced with an angry hiss.

At this, Alison chuckled. "And what, pray tell, is to keep me from simply stamping you out of existence when I got there?"

You-You ... wouldn't ... dare! He gasped in utter disbelief.

"Oh, wouldn't I? Who's going to stop me? Huh?"

She felt the hotness of his anger wash over her as he fumed in silence.

"You?! Tell me, why exactly should I spare you? Give me one good reason." She was insulted that he had clearly not even considered the possibility.

You ... you fiend! You would simply destroy me!? Even I am not so cruel! It took an unneeded breath, in all likelihood for dramatic effect rather than out of habit. *If blood means nothing to you, then at least consider all the times I have saved your skin since our coming here.* True, he had helped her dodge a situation or two in the past, but it was still hard to say whether it made up for the rest of the troubles he had caused.

Honestly, I do not know how you have survived the number of times you have drank yourself into oblivion, or worse. All I can do is watch as you wreak your havoc.

"Well, maybe if you would just shut up every once in a while, I wouldn't have to drink so try so hard to drown you out!"

It was then that Alice noticed the golden glint of something resting just under the edge of the gargantuan trash receptacle. *What the hell else am I supposed to do in here?! All you ever do is ignore me, anyway* ... Her tight denim skirt pressed uncomfortably against her thighs as she leaned down to take a closer look. *Are you even listening to me!?* Now he was shrill with exasperation. *Seriously ... again? This is exactly what I am talking about!*

Upon further inspection it became clear from the distinctive blue stripes that the glint was coming from a photo ID. *Hellooooo?* She heard his ever-needy chiding, but it was muffled as if in the distance as Alice tried to wedge her arm under the dumpster.

"Now, if I can just reach it ..." She stretched her arm as far as she could possibly reach. The pavement dug uncomfortably into her bony knees, and the breeze left her backside feeling a little more exposed than she liked, but as she grunted with effort, the tips of her fingers finally managed to scrape the card just close enough to grab the edge.

She pulled it out gingerly, being careful to touch as little of the card as possible. She vaguely heard the sound of the voice whining in the background, but all was silent in her mind as she confirmed that the picture on the ID was indeed that of her quarry.

"So, he was here ..." She was glad to have at least confirmed that much, but she wasn't left with much to go on. The GPS signal had cut out a short distance from this very spot, and nobody seemed to have seen Kumo after he left the train stop.

Alice carefully dropped the ID into her breast pocket and gracefully pushed herself upright. She smoothed her skirt back down across her thighs and walked slowly back to the train station.

What are you planning? You could at least keep me in the loop. The voice had calmed noticeably at the sign of progress.

"We are going to find him yet, and as long as you don't do anything stupid, there is a chance I will let you live."

I am guessing that is the best you will offer, so I suppose I will take it. If you want to play with that pet of yours, fine, but I want nothing to do with it.

For once both seemed satisfied, and she was left to carry on the rest of the way in relative silence as she tried to plan what was to come.

BITTER REFLECTIONS

It had taken some time to drag himself from the forest—the forest where he would have gladly taken his last breath, if it were not for what little honor was left in him.

Instead, he stood in the bathroom of the now-abandoned warehouse that he for so long had known as something of a second home. It seemed the mirror before him mocked him. It felt as though even it could see the truth, and what it now cast back disgusted him greatly. The boy with long, curling brown hair, smooth unblemished tan skin ... but that was not the half of it. The thing that stared back at him—it smiled; its teeth glared in the darkness as the ridges of its mouth grew farther and farther apart until he could no longer bear it.

His nostrils flared in anger, and with a terrible rage he hurled his fist into the terrible image's center. He watched as blood dripped down the hundreds of cracks that now spread from where his knuckles rested. But still before him lay a creature he never wished to see again.

He closed his eyes and allowed for one deep breath. "Erased ..." His fists clenched tighter as he spoke. "You must be erased." As he slowly uttered those words, a resolve grew inside him, and his fingers began to pry from beneath their reflection a blood-soaked sliver of glass. His eyes opened, and there was a manic rage in them. "None will know you as you once were, or as you are now. You will be forgotten ... *replaced*."

And so the man brought the bloody shard to his brow and began his repentance. One handful at a time, he cut away the curls he had no right to. On into the night he tore and cut, until finally what lay before him in the shattered mirror was so mutilated that not even he could find the reflection he had once known. All that was left of him were his eyes, and though he tried, he could not bring himself to take them. In the end, he decided it would be too kind a fate for him never again to see the eyes of that whom he hated most ... himself.

There he stood locked in his own hateful gaze. His eyes still locked, he dropped the blood-soaked shard of glass into the sink where it cracked and slid to the bottom of the pile of blood and hair.

"Noxia," he growled through gritted teeth. He repeated the word over and over as he reached his shaking hand to his blood-soaked brow and wrote in large manic print over his face: N O X I A. He continued to repeat the word under his breath and wrote the letters over and over until his face was obscured.

Finally, satisfied in his own pain, the man carried his tattered frame out into the open warehouse and made his way to the circle drawn at its center. There, he came upon his master, who lay crumpled and charred in a lifeless heap on the ground. He watched as the blood dripped down his chin and trickled gradually to his fingertips.

"Master ... what have I done?" Wish for it though he did, no answer came. The man who had stood by his side all of these years, who had taught him all that he knew, now lay dead before him. Accident or not, he could do little to escape the fact that it had been his fault.

"Come, let us journey once more together ... Your place of honor awaits you." His words came after what seemed an eternity of silence and were full of a terrible pain and duty. A pain made only worse by the emptiness in him that grew as he knelt beside the man he had known and loved as a father, the man who had been so good to his former self. What lay before him was but the empty husk of what once was, but that knowledge gave him little comfort as he slowly dragged his master across the cold concrete floor. Indeed ... there was little comfort in this.

ΔΔΔ

It had been several hours since he had loaded his master's remains into the rickety old handcart. Its wheels had clattered, and its frame had creaked in protest as they made their journey along the dark unpaved streets on the outskirts of Tidworth and Andover.

Behind him there rose a large black column of smoke high into the early morning skyline. The growing flames rose high enough that just the tips could be seen, even some miles in the distance.

So far, he had made good time on the first fifteen miles of the long journey he had resolved to make on foot in solemn penance. The smell of burnt flesh wafted along with nauseating fury—a constant reminder of the silent companion who rode in the flimsy conveyance his bloodied hands dragged wearily behind him. He knew he would have to do something about the smell soon, but for the time being, the only vehicles that had gone by had been firefighters rushing past him in the opposite direction, and they had other things to worry about. And so, he decided to endure the bitter proof of his deed.

Time went on with little in the way of events for a good number of hours. There was, of course, the company of his ever-protesting cart, and the occasional ripple of leaves in the forest, but all in all his company was that of silence and sorrow. He carried on this way until, in complete exhaustion, he found himself dragging his burden into the backwoods of Axford, an hour's walk from the south edge of Basingstoke. Here he slumped in a miserable heap against the cart's muddy wheels, praying for the darkness of sleep to take him as he watched the black column that still lingered far in the distance.

His aching body soon found rest, but fate was not so kind as to grant him a dreamless sleep as he lay perfectly still in his silent torment while the sun was slowly obscured by the storm clouds that drifted in from the east.

A SOLEMN DUTY

It was with a heavy heart that Khalos slowly packed his belongings into a small black duffel. The weight of responsibility for his men had never seemed heavier than it did on this night. He had called each of them in turn and relayed the message, and though he hid it behind his air of confidence, he had never felt as helpless as he did upon issuing the command, knowing full well that he could provide no answers to the questions that would inevitably follow. So far, each in good faith had agreed to meet the call to action despite their reservations, but their questions gnawed at his soul, for they were as unanswerable as his own.

He lingered on the picture of his daughter, and for the first time, he let the tears flow as the thought of never seeing his five-month-old little girl again crossed his mind. His wife was used to him going on long "business" trips; she hadn't even complained when he let her know he would be gone for a few

144

weeks. Not that he had any idea how long it would really be, or if he would return at all.

So many questions, but the only answer he had to give was duty … duty to what? It had been so long since he had known any mission but to care for his family and to help his men to make lives of their own after the order had disbanded. Had the call come a few years earlier, he could think of more than a handful of men who would have still been eager for the life that they had left, but it was due much to Khalos's efforts to reintegrate his men that none had sounded eager upon hearing the news.

"You all but abandoned us, Dragon Lady," he muttered to himself as he finally managed to pull his gaze away from his daughter's photo. He knew it would only make things harder, but he could not let the precious image go, so he placed it gently into the duffel with the rest of his belongings.

It was strange to think how far he had come from the man he had once been. He remembered his younger days in which he and Göttrick had spent every waking moment in competition for the Dragon Lady's attentions. There certainly had been a time when that would truly have been all that mattered to him, but that time had apparently passed. He hadn't felt it go, but clearly it had slipped through his fingers, and now he stood here fumbling through the trinkets of the new life he had made for himself while he prepared to return to the old life that had abandoned him.

Göttrick and the Dragon Lady had not made this life—no, it was he who had found love; it was he who had brought his two children into this world. And now it was he who sat planning to leave them for who knows what errand.

He could not bear to think of his life without his children in it, but try though he might, he could not force the thought from his mind. Some time ago, his sense of honor had been replaced by his sense of duty to family—and the displaced soldiers at his command. He imagined their pain as each of his men now readied to leave their families. He cursed his own name that he had been the one who guided them into this new way of life and that now he was the one to tear it away.

Having put together the rest of his belongings, he reluctantly pulled Ásgeirr's long curved blade from the display case, where it had long hidden in plain sight, over his old cherrywood desk. Sheathing the sharp katana's blade, he placed it gently atop the rest of his equipment. With a final glance at the memories that hung around him, Khalos zipped up his duffel. He walked slowly down the dark hallway, gently touching his son's doorway as he passed it. On he pressed until he finally came to his bedroom door. There he waited quietly as he pulled himself together for the task that lay ahead.

Finally, he crept into the room where his wife's sleeping silhouette was the first thing to greet him. Before moving any farther forward, he turned to the bassinet where his daughter's tiny frame lay in a quiet and peaceful sleep. "Be strong, my young one." He pressed his lips to her forehead and listened to her gentle breath as it passed from her tiny lips. "I promise I will return to you."

"Is that you, dear?" his wife murmured as she was stirred from her slumber. "Come to bed already, love; it's the middle of the night. Your work can wait 'til morning."

At that, he took his lips from his daughter's forehead, sighing heavily as he passed the point where he could feel her breath upon his skin. "Yes, you are right, dear ... it can wait until tomorrow," he whispered, more to himself than to anyone else, as he made his way to fill the emptiness beside her. Though it brought him only a little comfort, he tried to content himself in the knowledge that there would be one more night in his wife's warm embrace.

LOST SOUL

Meanwhile, the broken man who had been asleep in the forest finally stirred. The power with which the stench now rolled up out of the handcart to assault his nostrils made it abundantly clear that it was past noon and the sun was out. And though he had refused to open his eyes for over an hour, he was making little progress at imagining it all away.

So, with a heavy sigh, he pulled himself up, and as he did so, he felt the terrible physical pain that was the fruit of his many labors. His freshly scabbed head had burnt in the noonday sun, along with his master's now-stinking corpse. The darkening clouds had since moved in overhead, and drops of rain had just begun to fall. His back and feet ached from the many hours of travel, and his fingers throbbed from clutching the cart's handle. It was almost enough to bring him to his knees, but he managed to steady himself after a groan of pain.

He shook his head painfully, as the scent of decay hit his nostrils again. "It would seem that something must be done about this, master. Forgive me ..." his voice now barely a whisper as he lifted the gray blanket from his master's corpse. He stood for some time in silence, building resolve for what he had to do next.

He reached out and placed a hand on his master's charred feet, cringing slightly as he touched them. He widened his stance and brought his other hand to his chest as he did so.

"*Glaciem absorbeat hanc corpus inane.*" As he slowly spoke these words, cold air began to rise up from his hands, which now glowed light blue. "*Omnia servare tangis.*" The cold spread from his hands to halfway up the burnt body of his master. There was a continuous sound much like that of ice cubes crackling after being dropped in a fresh glass of warm water. "*Absorbeat eum glácies.*" His master's whole body now glowed light blue, and white cloudy plumes of fog rolled off the inch-thick sheet of ice that enveloped him.

Though the stench of death still lingered in the air, it no longer arose from the body before him, and that was all he needed. And so the man closed his eyes and pried his frosty hand from the frozen corpse before him. His hand had accumulated a few centimeters of ice, but, in a flash of steam, it was once again his own. Now, he was able to breathe more easily; with great relief, he placed the shroud back over his master, where it belonged.

"Come, master. We've a long journey before us still." And so the young man threw his hood over his blood-encrusted face, wrapped his aching fingers one by one around the timeworn handle of the cart, and slowly made his way out of the forest. His feet sunk tiresomely into the thick mud, making his journey all the more befitting of its penitential purpose.

He was careful to think only of the next step, one after another. He tried to focus on the pain in his body as he trudged onward, against the will of his weary muscles and bones. He hoped somehow that one pain could ease the deeper pain that burned inside him, and for the time it did just that. He hoped, though he deserved not to live, that at least his actions now could serve his master.

So he trudged slowly on, through mile after mile of ever-wetter countryside, as he made his way down Salisbury Road. A thin line of asphalt cut through the forest that loomed overhead as it stretched southward for what seemed an eternity. The few cars that came upon him swerved and blared their horns as they angrily passed the unexpected obstruction to their journey. Once or twice a vehicle passed slowly; one even stopped to offer assistance. It took little more than a glimpse of the face hidden behind the cloak, however, for each to change their minds and speed quickly off into the distance toward the A303, where it would not be long before he joined them.

He did not know exactly what he would do after he arrived at his destination, but he knew that all who had preceded him and his master had been buried there. So, whatever it took, his master, too, would have his place next to the great masters of old.

SANGUINE TEARS

Though he could see nothing in the utter darkness that surrounded him, he could feel the cold metal as it cut into his wrists; he could hear the muffled echo of screams as the boy was tortured yet again.

"Answer the question!"

"Please, I don't know nothin'!" There was a gasp followed by an agonized howl of pain that rang out chillingly.

"You bring this on yourself, boy. Tell me where you hid it, or it'll be your brother who suffers next." The voice was full of a familiar uncaring menace that sent chills up Kumo's spine.

He had lost all sense of time down here—well, wherever *here* was—though he felt pretty certain that here was down. That, of course, was the only thing of which he felt certain anymore.

He had awoken this way at least a dozen times now—bound to the cold stone walls that seemed to be closing in around him, unable to cry out because of the stinking rag upon which he choked.

It had been difficult getting through the "conversations" up to this point, but he was learning that he was capable of enduring a lot more pain than he had previously thought. You see, he was learning how to separate himself from ... well, himself.

It's hard to explain, but I am sure you understand if you have ever experienced the kind of pain and fear that Kumo, trapped and tortured in the darkness, felt in those weeks.

Even now things seemed hazy in his mind. He had heard the interrogator's favorite inquiry about the whole "ring" bit hundreds of times. "We must have the ring, boy!" he would shout, and the boy would respond in what would seem almost genuine confusion, "What ring? There ain't no ring!" which of course would be followed by some obligatory screaming, and then he would move on to the part where he went into detail about the boy's uselessness.

Though he didn't like to admit it, ring or not, Kumo felt sorry for the kid. Hell, if the end of the boy's turn hadn't meant the beginning of his own, he would have hoped for it. As it was, though, Kumo had to be glad that there was someone else to take up some of the torturer's time and attention.

Kumo's mind drifted, as it often did, to thoughts of Alice, and for a moment, he was happy. Then, however, he heard the unmistakable sound of his fellow inmate's ragged body scraping on the concrete as it was dragged remorselessly back to its post. Before long, he felt his captor's breath fall heavily on his torn skin, a terrible fear filling him despite his best efforts, as he too was ripped from where he hung to be dragged just as helplessly along the frigid prison floor.

This part always seemed to last forever. He was getting used to the burning in his left hand, and though it grew fiercer, shooting down from his index finger, it was the least of his worries as his destination grew inevitably nearer.

He felt himself lifted into the air and dropped into the familiar embrace of the wintry steel of the interrogation chair. He was blinded by the bright light as the burlap sack was ripped ruthlessly from his blood-caked brow.

As his eyes adjusted, he could see the man with whom he had spent a great deal of his time lately. He stood, as usual, silhouetted by the unnervingly bright light that blazed behind him, wearing what looked to be a rather expensive suit. From his hand dangled the ever-familiar pendant he had only just received before this unlucky encounter.

"Now ... I am going to ask you one more time."

The man removed the rag from Kumo's mouth as he spoke. "Where did you get this?"

Kumo's mouth was terribly dry. It took a moment before he was able to speak. "I told you. I found it."

The man slapped him hard across the face, which was no surprise, as this was a familiar response to his usual reply.

"And would you happen to remember today where you found this most rare of treasures?"

"Perhaps, if my head was struck less often, I would find it easier to remember."

"You insolent fool!"

Kumo found the torture easier to endure this way; his "insolence," as the man always called it, was the only power he had anymore, the only path left to him for resistance.

"I'll have you know that we have it on good authority that the lady this belonged to was looking for a ring very much like the one you say our lad made off with."

He had tried—he really had—to protect her; he had never said a word about her throughout all the torture. How could they have found out about her? His eyes widened in horror. "Wha-?"

No—I must protect her, he thought. *But how?* His mind was a frantic mess of desperately dwindling hopes. One by one they were all falling away, leaving him with nothing to hold onto. Soon his despair would be so great that there could be no return.

A manic smile spread over the man's face. "Thank you for confirming. Never can be too sure about the help these days." He spun the pendant absentmindedly as he spoke.

"Don't you dare lay a finger on her!" There was a desperation in his voice the likes of which his interrogator had only dreamed of hearing until this moment.

"That is none of your concern now." Finally, the satisfaction he craved. "I think perhaps our conversations have come to a convenient ending point." He drew from the table that was littered with his favorite implements of pain a tool he had yet to have had the pleasure of using thus far in their sessions, a device which would mean the end, but a favorite nonetheless.

A terrible conflict brewed in Kumo's mind. On the one hand, this was the moment he had so often prayed for, an end to the insufferable pain, an end to the terrible fear that consumed him each day. On the other, he still hoped that he could serve as a distraction to keep this blackguard away from Alice, that his suffering could have at least some meaning. As he watched the long rusty blade ascend over his captor's shoulders, he finally felt that hope snuffed out.

"It seems your usefulness has run out."

As the blade finally descended, Kumo shut his eyes and, for the first time, wondered briefly what lay beyond the rift.

ΔΔΔ

What is going on? I should be dead. Am I? Is this what lies after? Kumo ventured a glimpse at his surroundings.

There was something wrong with this picture, very wrong. His captor's manic grin had turned to an expression of genuine bewilderment. And then Kumo saw it: the blood seeping from a thin line at his abuser's neck, just before the man tumbled to the ground, his head rolling off into the shadows.

A new figure stood before Kumo. Its armor was much like that of those who guarded "The Wall," except that its metal plates were stained the blackest of blacks. Where it differed the most, however, was in its blood-stained cowl. Were he not already expecting death, he would likely have been even more terrified by this unknown personage than he had been of his torturer. Jagged teeth gleamed with sinister purpose from under the flaring nostrils of a long dragon-like snout that spewed plumes of white smoke. It was a fearsome sight.

"Are you alright?" the voice behind the mask asked. Did Kumo hear some compassion in the question? Perhaps he was mistaken; it had been a long while since he had heard anything like kindness. The voice, though, did somehow seem ... familiar. Could it be ...?

It was all too much to take in; he hadn't been prepared for hope. He hadn't been ready for saving. He had only just come to terms with his death.

"It-It's me, Kuve. It's Alice." She pulled the garish mask from her face, revealing the puffy, red, teary eyes that hid beneath. "Please! Tell me you're okay, Kuve!"

"Alice? It's really you?" Could he trust this? He didn't know if he could bear it if this turned out to be his mind playing tricks on him.

"Of course it is, dear." He couldn't be sure, but he felt as though his wrists and feet had been freed from their bindings. He wasn't ready, though, to turn his gaze away from her face to find out.

"Please ... Don't leave me."

"I promise that I will never leave you again."

He felt her wrap gently around him as she carefully lifted him. Felt the warmth of her cheek against his own. For the first time, he dared to believe this was real, and tears streamed down his face. Tears that mingled with hers.

Peace washed over him as he was relieved of the duty of consciousness. He only just managed to utter "The boy …" before he took his rest.

NO SIMPLE STORY

Alison had not expected things to be so terribly difficult; not anticipated Kumo's absence from his humble abode; not predicted his disappearance from the train; had not a forecast of the time it would take to track him down. All this had passed, but now she found, as she held him close against her breast, she could not have understood the passion with which she sought to find him—not until this irrefutable moment of clarity—clarity that no mere nagging voice in her head could hope to eviscerate.

He seemed so much thinner ... so much frailer than she remembered him—if that was indeed possible. She looked down at the bloody stream of tears drying on his paler-than-pale face.

"I promise ... I will never leave you again," she repeated softly in his ears as she signaled for her men.

"You. The boy," she pointed, and without hesitation one of the six sentinels in her entourage flew into the darkness. The pickings for her guard had been slimmer than she had hoped, but luckily these few had at least maintained themselves in her absence.

"The rest of you know what to do." At that, four more broke off, making haste to remove all evidence that their party had been there.

"It is done, my lady." It was the voice of the most loyal of her guard as he returned from the other cell, carrying the small boy in his arms.

"Thank you, Göttrick."

"If you please, my lady, you are burdened. Let me get you some assistance."

"This burden is mine to be had."

Göttrick paused, but then he grunted in understanding.

As she turned, she stopped suddenly in her tracks and reached down to rip something that glinted even in the darkness from the limp hands of her burden's would-be murderer.

Satisfied, she stood and made her way up the rickety stairs that led to the first floor of the abandoned apartment building. Kumo barely stirred as she carried him cautiously through the cobweb-ridden halls. They passed several Yakuza who lay slumped awkwardly against the walls, posing no danger to her party, as they had already been dealt with. Of course, she could barely recall anything she saw there as they made their way into the empty Kyokuto-Kai back alley.

"Your orders, m'lady?" The handful of men had returned to Alison, standing in formation, with the most senior of them addressing her. Clearly, they had finished their business inside.

"Burn it. Leave nothing standing."

"… Understood." There was a moment just then, a hesitation most unsettling—however brief it might have been. Even so, the small force dispersed as their leader spoke, each man executing his part as though performing a perfectly choreographed dance.

Alison said nothing aloud, though she made note of her man's pause. There will be time to deal with that matter later, she thought, as she slipped into the sleek silver sedan, gingerly strapping her companion in before taking up her place beside him. Göttrick had already set within the gangly mess of a boy he had delivered from the dungeon.

Neither Alison nor the voice who traveled via Alison's physical form spoke as the car merged onto the crowded streets of Tokyo, though they both gazed anxiously at the reflected pillars of smoke and flames that rose ominously in the distance behind them.

Eventually, the voice stated matter-of-factly, clearly not bothered in the slightest by the revelation, *This will mean a war, you know.*

"I do," Alison responded.

ΔΔΔ

Only minutes had passed before Alison found herself carrying Kumo aboard the 座礁ワン (*The Stranded One*). Upon recognition of their mistress and her burden, two of her men rushed forward to offer assistance. Göttrick held up his hand, halting them, and shook his head, indicating clearly that their services—however appreciated—would not be required. Instead, he directed them to ready the

167

ship for departure, and they scurried down to the dock to do their part.

Alison's and Göttrick's paths split when they reached the stairwell that led to the upper and lower decks of the ship. Where Göttrick took the boy to the infirmary on the main deck, Alice made her way to her quarters on the lower.

When she reached her room, she was glad to see that it had been outfitted as she had asked. There was a full stock of medical supplies in a cart that stood next to her bed.

And why exactly couldn't you have just tossed him to the infirmary like the other vagrant?

She ignored the voice as she gently draped Kumo's body over the pearly white of her bedsheets.

"It is worse than I thought." She took a deep breath as she absorbed the gravity of his afflictions.

The man who lay before her was in a terrible state. The soles of his feet were covered with a mixture of black soot and blood that only half obscured their many blisters. The few toenails he had were stained crimson and mangled; the rest presumably had been ripped viciously from their beds by rusty pliers, if not some more wicked implement. Her eyes scanned the gouges on his legs that could easily be seen through the tattered remnants of his slacks, then turned to the large bruises on his shirtless stomach. She lingered over the finger marks that appeared so clearly around his throat and then, the source of those sanguine tears, the dozens of gashes that enshrouded what once had been the lids of his eyes.

What filled her was a mixture of sadness and rage as she prepared his arm and deftly inserted the IV needle that led to a bag of saline. Kumo's shallow breathing was briefly elevated, but as the trickle of morphine joined the flow, it was not long before it had returned to its prior state.

This would have been much easier if you had just let them off him. Which, might I add, was my suggestion in the first place. The voice offered more of his snide commentary.

"Shut up!" She tore away her cumbersome armor and knelt beside Kumo in her pure white kimono, fighting against all odds to hold at bay the tears that welled up inside her.

You know, it's not too late. I can do it for you, if you like. You wouldn't even have to watch.

"Don't you dare!" For the first time, she noticed she was staring at something. Her covetous eyes were fixed upon the hand held firmly by her own, the hand whose nail-less index finger bore a mark made by a force entirely different from that of his afflictions. "Just shut up! I don't give a rat's left butt cheek what you think!"

She growled angrily at herself as, after what seemed an eternity, she managed to loosen her grip, allowing his palm to land softly beside her. Finally—though she did have her doubts—she felt almost ready to begin the colossal task of returning him to some semblance of what he had once been.

Though her shaking hands did their best to sew thread after thread after thread to close his wounds, it seemed her labors would never see their end.

The night wore slowly on as her vision was clouded by tears that came in bouts. She could not help the terrible and overwhelming sorrow that overcame her as she examined each and every injury that had been inflicted upon him.

"All this, for what!? All for the sake of finding me?" Her mind's wailing—should anyone have heard it— would have been a most pitiable sound indeed.

Now, now, my dear. There is no sense in blaming yourself for this.

"But it is my fault! I never should have given him that trinket."

Finally! Something upon which we can agree!

"Don't let that coincidence go to your head." Alice did her best to put the unpleasant revelation from her mind as she grumpily resumed her labors.

Alright, I do admit that I had only our interests in mind. Still, I did warn you to leave things be. Remember, I told you, "Only a ..."

"... fool would risk so much for nothing." Her fists clenched, and she ground her teeth as she spoke, "I know what you told me, you heartless bastard!"

All I do is help, and yet it would seem I will never win your favor.

"Oh really? Now what on earth would make you think that!?" She took a deep breath, relaxed her fists, and continued with renewed fervor in the devotion given to the task at hand.

Well, then, that is better! It would appear my work here is done. You are welcome—by the way.

Though she had resolved to ignore any further interruption by the voice's nonsense, ignoring the vexation that filled her at his words seemed simply impossible. Her nose wrinkled up, and her eyebrows arched quizzically. "Uh, what exactly did I miss? Last I checked, the only contribution you have made has been to the foulness of my mood!" She stuck out her tongue in a most indignant gesture as her challenge sprang sarcastically from her grimacing lips.

What, you haven't noticed the improvement? Look how much better those stitches are coming now. He laughed with a touch more mania than necessary. *Heaven knows, I would much rather help a bit than endure the many, many*—he paused, as if to breathe—*many unbearably dreary years I would be damned to spend listening to the pathetic whining that would surely ensue were anything to befall the miserable shadow of a man with whom you have clearly developed an ill-advised infatuation.*

Alice was dumbfounded into silence. It was true; Kumo would likely be grateful for the renewal of her hands' former skill, but more important was the sudden realization of how unusually attached she had really become. This, of course, just made her puff up angrily; she didn't like being the last one to notice something, particularly something about herself.

In any case, after much deliberation, I have decided—at least for now—that it may be to our mutual benefit if I let you keep this one alive.

This proclamation was most unexpected, most unexpected indeed. "You mean—"

Yes, yes. I suppose I shan't try to kill him again anytime soon ... if it is soooo terribly important to you.

All in all, a bit dramatic, but the best she could honestly have hoped for. Better, perhaps.

"Well, ummm—thanks, I guess." She was not entirely relieved by his assurances, but it would certainly be enough to get her through the night.

THE TOLL

Alice was still sewing. It seemed as if days and days had passed. Every time she finished mending one terrible gash, it seemed another she had not seen was revealed. It was her suspicion that her efforts were being undone by some mysterious force.

"Verdammen Sie es!" she cursed angrily in German as she watched her efforts slowly unwinding before her eyes.

"I knew it!" She made to grab the thread that seemed to crawl from his flesh of its own power, but as she took hold of one of its wriggling ends, it writhed with unexpected fury.

And then, to her horror, all at once the stitches began to rip angrily from his flesh, tearing new wounds as they flew from those they bound together.

Suddenly, Kumo's lids shot open to reveal two gaping holes from which a thousand throbbing blood-soaked threads began to squirm, and then it came ... The blood-curdling scream that threatened to rend her soul into nothingness.

"Noooo!" The thread had escaped her grasp and was now crawling insolently up his torso.

There was a sudden loud crashing—the thud thud thud of metal, but that mattered little.

Try though she might, she could not stop the thread that slithered slyly across him, stopping only once it had reached his neck.

Thud thud thud—the strange sound grew louder now ... closer.

The thread reared up threateningly, revealing its wicked plot as it grazed the tip of its sharp needle against Kumo's skin ... blood dripping in its wake.

"Noooo! Not him! Take me in his place! Ple—" Something had her, its claws pressed hard upon her shoulders, tearing her from this world.

ΔΔΔ

She woke with a start, winded by the terror that had filled her. It was all she could do to gather strength for one long painful breath.

Alison found herself on the floor next to the bed. She pulled the covers hurriedly from atop Kumo, who lay bare beneath them. To her relief, each stitch was held firmly in its place, and though she could not for the life of her remember having finished, clearly she had somehow managed.

"Thank god." She returned the covers to their place and watched for a moment as they slowly rose and fell to the rhythm of his gentle breathing.

You could thank me. I did a lot more, the voice chided her, more playfully than usual.

She barely even noticed the complaint as a great peace had filled her as she watched him slowly breathing before her. It was midday by the looks of the bright light that poured in from the porthole above them. Looking up, she noticed the bag that had held his saline solution hung limply, crumpled by the vacuum of nothingness as it had emptied through the night. She made a mental note to change it the moment she got the energy to come to her feet.

Again the room was filled with the same ominous *thud thud thud* of her dream, but being of a clearer state of mind now, she realized that this was someone at her door.

"Yes?" she croaked through her cracked lips, the dryness of which surprised her.

"M'lady! Is everything alright?" Göttrick's voice showed true concern. A wave of embarrassment shot through her, and she could feel her face burning as she realized that she must have been talking—or rather shouting—in her sleep.

"No need to worry, Göttrick, it was just a bad dream." She did her best to sound as calm as possible. Well, a terrible horrible nightmare really, she thought, but that bit she chose not to trouble him with; though she had more than a sneaking suspicion that he had already deduced as much from whatever utterances she had made as she slumbered.

"You are certain, m'lady?"

"Yes, yes. Thank you, Göttrick. I shall meet you on the deck shortly."

"Very well, m'lady." Apparently satisfied, Göttrick returned to his usual tone of formality.

She listened as the gentle rustle of his armor faded into the distance before deciding to try her luck at standing. As she did so, a terrible pain shot through both her legs, an unfortunate consequence of spending over fourteen hours resting upon the hard floor.

"I suppose I should consider myself lucky to feel them at all." She groaned as her limbs struggled against her efforts to move them.

You should indeed!

"Oh, you're still here. Good morning ... I guess." She had almost forgotten her needy tagalong and wasn't exactly glad for the company.

Now, now, that's no way to greet an old friend. Plus, you may have missed it, but morning has left us already.

"Eh, sorry. I'm not feeling particularly chatty at the moment." She had managed to replace the bag of saline and now began the chore of checking Kumo's wounds for seepage. In all honesty, she would likely have found any other mundane task that needed doing if it meant an excuse not to hear her constant companion prattle on about whatever he fancied being offended by today.

That I noticed. Well, I suppose I have little to say in any case. Just trying to be polite, you know.

"Alright, that's it! What the hell is up with you? All this 'Just trying to be polite, you know' and this whole 'mutual benefit' business. What exactly are you scheming?"

Scheming? Me? Cannot one simply wish you a good morning?

"Oh, come on! You are not 'one,' you are you, and in all the many years you have graced me with your presence, not once have you been so pleasant for the simple sake of being so."

Well, perhaps, I have changed. His tone brought the image of a petulant child to Alison's mind.

"Perhaps ... Time will tell." She most certainly could not believe it possible, but she wanted an end to the conversation, so she let it go. She had other things to take care of. She exchanged her blood-soaked kimono for a clean one, then donned her armor and went above.

Göttrick stood watch upon the ship's stern, his wavy blond hair whipping in the salty sea breeze that carried the aroma of freshly caught salmon to

Alison's nose. His hands lay firmly upon the rails as he scanned the horizon for any hint of trouble.

"Ever the diligent one, aren't we? You know, we have radar doing that work for you now, Göttrick." She knew he knew this, but she so enjoyed poking fun at him.

"Ah, m'lady, many apologies. Old habits, you know." He bowed his head apologetically as he turned to face her.

"It is perfectly alright. Just know I would not hold it against you if you chose to spend your time in some other way. Anyway, what is our status?" She smiled reassuringly at him as she spoke, even going so far as to bat her eyelashes a little, despite it being neither appropriate nor needed—force of habit, you know.

Göttrick stood at attention as he replied, "I am pleased to report that we have managed to put over a hundred more kilometers of ocean between us and the mainland than we had previously anticipated. That puts us at approximately seven hours before we land in Naha."

"Good, good! I am glad that everything is going smoothly."

His brow furrowed as again his head bowed in shame. "Well, not everything, m'lady."

"Oh?"

"Well, you see, we have been following the chatter, and it seems last night's tactics were not entirely appreciated. An army of vessels mounts against us from either direction as we speak." It was clear from his expression that he had hoped to avoid having to deliver this news to his mistress, had hoped for some reversal of their fortunes that had failed to materialize.

"I see." She frowned at his words, but then remembering that it was she who had ordered that she was not to be disturbed for any reason, she stifled her anger. "Do you have their positions?"

"Yes, m'lady. Additionally, we have taken great pains to gather all information available on each vessel. Would you care to join me at the helm for a full briefing?"

She gave a nod of confirmation. Then, both fastened their cowls in place, their solemn expressions safely hidden behind the frozen faces they wore; they began their deliberate march to the command center that lay at the ship's highest reaches.

"M'lady, there is one more thing. It is the crew." Göttrick spoke softly, to avoid being overheard.

"Yes, what of them?"

"I fear not all have taken to these long weeks at sea." It was clear from his body language that he was ashamed of what he needed to relay to his mistress about the men under his command, though he tried his best to keep his manner matter-of-fact.

"I see." The suspicion that had been steadily brewing in her mind was thus confirmed.

"M'lady, I beg your pardon, but they hear your screams in the night—I have no power to prevent it anymore. Their faith is stirred by the change that has come upon you." There was great concern in his voice. "I fear the worst, m'lady. What would you have me do?"

"We must be watchful; we must be ever wary; but above all, we must proceed with the certainty that the path we tread leads us still toward our journey's end." She placed her hand comfortingly upon his shoulder. "And, with that in mind, let us tend to the dreary business of these Yakuza scum who lack the good sense that keeps most respectable noses far from business in which they shouldn't sniff around." They continued their trek up the stairs that led to the upper decks, showing no evidence in their stride of the matters that taxed them so heavily.

TAKING OUT THE TRASH

Alison stood admiring the circular radar screen in the middle of the command center. The device was made to her specifications, and by request it worked much as a traditional map table did when battles needed planning. It was a small joy, but she loved to watch the little ships dragged slowly across the surface of its screen by way of a network of computer-controlled magnets that lay below.

Göttrick stood beside her, going over the ins and outs of the whole nasty business of their enemy's steady approach. All the while, though she listened, Alice mostly watched intently as the tiny hand-painted copy of her ship slowly edged closer to its destination. There were more than a dozen ships on its tail, and at least one more standing by at each of the six major islands of lower Japan. Naturally, Okinawa—Alison's intended destination—had more enemy ships waiting, six vessels in all.

To the untrained eye, the ships were all civilian and private fishing vessels, but careful data collection and observation made it possible to identify which ships were potential threats, and likely owned by the Yakuza.

"Has the dinghy been outfitted as I asked?" She had interrupted Göttrick, but any more talk seemed a waste; she saw her strategy on the table before her.

"Yes, ma'am, we have installed the ship's beacon just as you requested." This was from the ship's engineer, though she had been addressing Göttrick. The boy was a younger, and less seasoned, member of the crew, one who clearly had yet to learn his place.

"And the jammers?" She did not acknowledge the boy's mistake, addressing Göttrick instead.

"Yes, ma'am! I tested them myself." The boy again spoke out of turn. It seemed his errancy would have to be corrected more directly. Alice frowned, knowing that Göttrick would read the slightest pursing of her lips as a sign to act on her behalf.

"LEARN YOUR PLACE, BOY!" Göttrick's voice was fierce; it was clear that further leniency on the matter would not be forthcoming. Finally realizing his error, the boy shrunk back into the corner, where he stared in silence at his feet.

"Jammers ready?" Alice asked again.

"They are, m'lady," Göttrick replied. He nodded at the engineer to resume his position.

The boy stepped forward without a sound, ready to act upon his mistress's word.

"On my mark. In five."

"Four."

"Three."

"Two."

"One." And the boy was at it with the flipping of switches and the twisting of dials.

The map table had hitherto been covered by green blobs that drifted across the ocean, attending mostly to their own dull business. For the most part, each blob was accompanied by a tiny impersonator of the ship it represented; there were, though, those unlucky few who, being afforded no such honor, were condemned to roam the seas as lone blobs. Things had gone on this way for quite some time, but now there was a change. At first, the blobs grew fuzzy at their edges, and then the whole map was suddenly covered, every inch, by the confusing hail of returns that suddenly appeared—an unfortunate consequence to jamming all radar and beacon frequencies being that this also affected one's own picture of things.

"Now, the dinghy. Drop it!" This time only a single switch was flung, but she could hear the dinghy behind the ship as it crashed into the sea.

"Course?" Göttrick asked.

"Match it to our own." Alice was enjoying how well things were turning out so far.

"Understood."

And for several minutes they waited in silence. Alison moved to the plan's next phase only when she was satisfied that her assailants continued pursuit. "Now, take us due west, but leave the dinghy be."

Göttrick nodded and went to the wheel, where, by his hand, the boat was swiftly taken more than ninety degrees from its course. Much that was loose on the ship landed upon its floor as it seemed the vessel would surely capsize and be swallowed by the sea, but still the little hand-painted ship skidded slowly over the map's surface, its course unchanged. It continued upon the same route, as all the while the real ship with all its crew and cargo were taken farther and farther away by every moment's passing.

Alison watched in silence for several minutes as her pursuers drew ever closer to the inevitable disappointment that awaited them. The beacon transfer had been easy, but creating a radar signature for such a small dingy had been a more impressive feat. Given its ability to trick her own top-of-the-line monitoring system, the dinghy had no chance of being detected by the systems of her enemy.

"It seems things are in hand here. I shall check on our guests; notify me when we are ready to begin phase four," Alison ordered as she made her way from the helm, and though the crew seemed confused by her words, Göttrick nodded in affirmation.

Now, you might ask, as did her men, how is it that we come already to a fourth phase when no mention of a first, second, or third has been made?

The answer—Alison had, upon learning of Kumo's whereabouts, devised a plan of many phases that was imparted only to her general, and even then, the design was only revealed shortly before its swift execution began, and with great pains taken to maintain secrecy … given recent misgivings of some crew members.

Of course, the first matter attended to was never "official business," as that was the part in which she had leaked information about her amulet; the part in which she lay in wait and hoped against hope that watching the path that information took would lead her to where Kumo was being held. This matter Alison later affectionately dubbed "phase zero" of the undertaking.

As for phase one, that consisted of the dangerous foray into the foul-smelling slums from which Kumo was retrieved, the same foul-smelling slums that, consumed by flames, surely were no more, a warning to those who would dare to cross her.

Phase two brought mistress, crew, and guests to the vessel that now carried them to their destination.

Phase three began with buoys deployed to stymie any attempts at finding *The Stranded One* through echolocation and radar. These were equipped to efface any incoming sonic or radio waves, whether through air or water, and return only random noise. The sea surrounding the isles would remain a mysterious blank spot on the enemy's maps while these were active.

Phase three was twofold. The only frequencies left unmolested were those dedicated to the beacons mandated to operation on each ship that traveled these harbors. This was our brave dinghy's play. Having taken the enemy's eyes, rather than afford them reason to find and eliminate the interference at its source, Alison decided—and, it would seem quite rightly so—that if left with the knowledge of her whereabouts—albeit, false knowledge—they would continue their pursuit.

Thus far, each phase had come to pass without a hitch, but if ever they should dock in Naha, they would need a little luck; phase four, hopefully, would bring it. As they approached, it was indeed possible that their salvation already lay in its place of designation, drifting leisurely, just northwest of the island city of Amami.

ΔΔΔ

Alison made haste to check on Kumo, worried that something might have fallen on him during that brazen maneuver. In her absence, the helm—previously the image of order—lay now in an uneasy state of unrest.

It is possible that the crew members, in their agitation, may have forgotten their general's continued (but silent) presence. Whatever the case, however, the dangerous words they spoke were leading them toward mutiny.

"What are we—weak children?" It was the voice of he who had hesitated at the burning of the enemy's slums, he who was directly under only General Göttrick and the Dragon Lady herself.

Several of the crew had stopped their business and listened in apparent agreement, nodding.

"Here we stand at the ready, her chosen ones. We are the unrelenting force that manifests her will. We have, in times past, laid waste to whole nations, if only she bade it so, and would again." He continued his speech, now the whole of the nearby crew abandoning their duties, drawing closer as he spoke; and though the general was ashamed, he too was drawn by his subordinate's words.

"Now we stand in the face of a mere handful of vessels that—armed poorly, if at all—stand only to fall at our hand. And, what is it we do? Do we honor ourselves, descended of the Ancients, trained in the ways of the 'Invincibles' as we have been? Do we now honor those that came before us?"

By this time all who gathered had become as ravenous dogs that pace and drool hungrily before the promise of a feast. The general did not join them, and yet spellbound as he was by talk of his own heritage, he was paralyzed by anticipation.

"Nay! I ask you, what honor is there in deception? None! I ask you, what honor can be found in retreat?"

All in the crowd grumbled in apparent agreement—all, it would seem, but one.

"The Dragon is not herself these days. You all have seen it! You have heard her fits in the night!

Witnessed this very day her unwillingness to act!" He paused, allowing them to process this sudden turn. Though several backed away in disbelief, there were none that could deny his words.

The chilling realization of the rabble-rouser's aim released the general from the state of numbness that had held him. He must find some opportunity to warn his mistress without being seen.

"The Dragon is unfit for her post, and if there is yet hope of honoring our ways, the ways of our ancestors before us, we would be wanting if we did nothing to relieve her of it." He held himself with the pleased surety that came as his carefully delivered call to insurgence garnered a terrible chorus of cheers that could lead only to one end.

While the traitor gave his call to action and received approval from the crowd, Göttrick had inched toward the exit. He was almost there when, it seemed, the rabble as one noticed him. Instantly, a terrible silence fell over all and no one moved a muscle. Göttrick and the mutineers found themselves locked tensely in each other's gaze, each man uncertain of what was to be the result of this unfortunate difference of opinion.

ΔΔΔ

Alison heard the clamor above her, the muffled cheers and jeering laughter, but thought nothing of it as she busied herself at Kumo's side. It was an unimportant matter, one easily attended to by her most trusted general.

She gingerly maneuvered Kumo's limp and helpless figure onto a litter, where she secured him for the pending transfer.

She held his hand, longing for him to wake and greet her, as their yacht flew them madly past the many isles of Japan, bringing them ever closer to the foray that awaited them.

CHG
COMPANY

There was a heavy fog over the lake, making it difficult to pin down exactly what time of day it was, but it was certainly bright enough to call it daytime. The rippleless gray mirror that lay at Kumo's feet—though it surely continued into infinity—faded quickly into the whiteness that enveloped everything that lay ahead.

The air was pleasantly cool, the water warm and welcoming as it passed between his toes that, dipping delightedly, left tiny streaking waves in their wake. The warmth of the water brought a steady roll of steam, the lake's generous contribution to the all-encompassing haze.

Kumo sat comfortably on the large pillowy loveseat, bobbing up and down as it floated, carrying him where'er it fancied to go. In his left hand, he held a leather pouch full of many different colored stones; from his right was flung a small red stone that skipped almost a dozen times before fading into obscurity.

Kumo had been here for some time now, and he had to say that it was not that shabby a place, really. Well, the view could stand some improvement, but, all in all, it was a nice place.

"Float, Float," he tossed another rock that skipped twice before it was lost in the murky depths below,

"My fluffy boat!

Onward carry me!

Ain't got no shoes!

Ain't got no socks!

Ain't naught here but we three!

Aye, a lusty soul,

This 'ere bag o' rocks,

And a boat built just for me!"

He was certainly no professionally trained artisan, and his English was pretty bad, but he had practiced this particular tune quite a lot lately, and so at least he didn't notice its imperfections any longer. Kumo took an exaggerated, and unnecessarily loud, breath and continued,

197

"Nary a soul,

Nary a soul,

Nary as merry as we!

Who fly o'er the waters,

Like wee little otters,

Beating our heads with our feet!"

By way of finale, he knocked his knuckles upon his brow, letting himself fall dramatically over the plush round leather arms of his floating throne, hanging his tongue out and rolling his eyes in the back of his head for good measure.

He lay there basking in the steam, which welled up in hot plumes that cleared his sinuses as he breathed them in. His silky hair lapped thirstily at the water's wetness, dipping in and out, swishing to and fro, all to the rise and fall of the water's whimsical swells.

It was calm—quiet—still, but for the rare sound of the water's splashing as it plunged to the depths below, having leapt from atop his head. Of course, if he listened hard enough, he could faintly hear a sound in the distance, though it was nearly imperceptible. It was the song made by a multitude of minuscule would-be waves that bounced impotently against his fluffy boat's brown suede skin. Finding only obliteration there, they each fizzled into nothingness, leaving but an echo of what they might have been in their wake—notes to be added to an endlessly futile song.

Then, there was a thunderous sound, a clapping that nearly startled Kumo straight from his skin and into the heavens, but he was relieved upon opening his eyes to find a familiar sight.

"Bravo! Bravo! Very good, m'lad!" Though he was upside down, it was clearly his good friend who greeted him so kindly from up on the red recliner that lay no more than a foot from Kumo's head.

"Remora! Where on earth have you been? And what's all that on your boat?" Kumo, who had pulled his tongue back into his head, first looked incredulously at the colonies of gray and black muck and mussels that, covering much of the recliner's lower half, were first to greet his blinking eyes. Having had his fill of the ghastly sight, he looked up at the upside-down man, who smiled brightly from his perch.

"I have brought you more stones, my boy! And as for me vessel—you've no business judging this 'ere," Remora lectured, wagging his finger playfully all the while. He did not wait for Kumo to sit up before tossing a heavy-looking satchel into his lap, where it landed with a rattle and a heavy thud. "There you are; you've run out."

Kumo, slightly winded, lurched up and gripped at his stomach. *What is he talking about?* he thought as he inspected the bag he'd been holding.

"So I have …" Kumo had recovered his breath only just enough to make the confused observation aloud; the bag, which he felt sure had just been full, indeed lay empty in his hands.

"A thank-you will do." There was just a hint of sternness in Remora's voice; he was apparently bothered by Kumo's continued ingratitude.

"Oh—ya, thanks!" Kumo shook his head dazedly and turned to face the middle-aged man who sat before him clad in thick leather and chain.

Their first meeting had come as Kumo slept in the room of a hundred thousand screens. And, though that fateful night in the strange wilderness of "The Wall" had been his last fleeting moments of happiness, Remora had been his dear and faithful companion ever since. His was the only light in the darkness of a most terrible and endless night. So much so that the thought of what nightmares might have found him in the absence of Remora's kindly presence sent shivers up Kumo's spine.

The crusty middle-aged man reached down the side of his red recliner and pulled at something. The recliner popped open, splashing water in Kumo's direction as Remora gave a happy sigh and settled back with his dripping legs propped up in the air.

"A grand day to be alive, my boy!" Remora exclaimed as he stretched his feet, cracking his toes and neck before allowing himself to sink all the way into relaxation. "Simply grand."

Kumo was green with envy at seeing Remora's recliner in action, but he decided it was better to let his petty jealousy pass without comment. Instead, he resumed his game, skipping a deep black stone as far as his eye could see. He simply gave a muffled "aye" in reply to his friend, otherwise content with silence.

It was some time before either interrupted the relaxation of their solitude, but when they did, it was Remora who first spoke.

"Pray, have I ever told ya of me young'uns?" Remora was feeling the twinge of pain that often bubbled forth when he was alone with his thoughts.

Kumo stopped mid-throw. "No. You've got kids?" Then, deciding it couldn't hurt, he threw the stone, anyway; it wasn't a terribly good throw, but that wasn't really important.

"Aye, two! Right little rascals, if I do say so myself," Remora's voice sounded both fond and forlorn.

"You really are an old man, Remora!" Both men laughed heartily.

"I suppose on that point I must concede, my boy!" Remora chuckled, glad to have Kumo for a distraction, but then he could not help but think of his children again. "They're still wee ones yet. The oldest not more than twenty seasons of age, while the youngest was born but seven moons ago."

"Okay, okay! So you're kinda old, but the longer you keep calling me *boy*, the less strength your arguments have." Of course, Kumo only half resented it. The honest truth was Remora was as close to a father figure as he had known for a very long time.

"Right you are, my boy! Right you are." Though the old man did his best to stifle it, Kumo could hear the slight waver in his voice.

"You cryin', old man? What's the matter?" Kumo had stopped tossing stones, deciding that it would be rude not to give the man his full attention.

"Oh, 'tis nothing. No need to trouble yourself with this old man's fragility," he said, but his voice sounded weepy as he spoke. "You see ... 'tis just that I miss them, the young'uns, me wife. Each of them feels so far away, as if they were but fading memories."

"I'm sorry. I didn't mean to be so insensitive," Kumo said, feeling rather like it was all his fault, whatever this place was, be it dream or reality.

Remora sniffled, taking a long shallow-sounding breath, "Not to worry, my boy! Do not go putting blame where blame does not belong, especially not on your very crown!" He exhaled deeply, his next breath sounding much healthier. "No, the matter is mine alone. Now, I managed some scouting. You ready to move on from this place?"

Kumo lifted up one foot from the water, inspecting it thoroughly. The foot was as plump and pruney as it had ever been, and upon further inspection, it appeared that bits of the very same muck that was growing on Remora's boat was starting on his soles. "I would say so." His voice carried some concern at the discovery of a barnacle between his toes.

Remora stretched his arms above his head, making a sound rather like that of a bear waking. And with a pull of the chair's side lever, there was a great splash as he shot upright once more, his legs plunged back into the water's murky depths.

"Right then. Catch." As he spoke, he tossed an old ruddy-looking oar toward Kumo's unsuspecting face; it was a miracle the boy managed to catch it with anything other than his all-too-trusting brow.

"Where to?" Kumo fumbled to get a grip on the oar before it was lost at sea; he had managed to deflect it from hitting him in the face but had not been quick enough to close his hands around it. It took him a moment to get properly settled.

"It is that strange place I spoke of before, the place of my waking that day we first met." Remora shivered as he thought of it. "I should warn you the place is dangerous. It is a right miracle I made it back in one piece, but if you are yet eager to see it ... I would rather like to have your take on the place. Perhaps, together, we might understand it better."

"Well, we certainly can't stay here any longer. Lead on, and where you go, I shall gladly follow."

Better with you than alone in this drear and empty sea, Kumo thought as they began their paddling in a direction that, as best they could guess, was somewhat northward.

As they paddled, there was a change in the wind. At first, it was subtle, little more than a stray drop falling here and there. As the fog thinned before them, however, the drops seemed to bring more and more of their friends with them until a torrential downpour was upon Kumo and Remora.

It was all they could do to keep themselves from being flung from their cushions as they navigated the ever-rising swells of the sea. Though Kumo had not been sure before, now he could taste it in the air: brine—this, surely, was no lake.

But they pressed on, Kumo with his mucky oar, Remora with his battle-worn broadsword, rowing ever farther from the brilliant light of day and the still waters they had known. Angry dark clouds beset them as they dashed through wave after wave. It seemed that they were being hunted by crash after thunderous crash of lightning, the strikes growing nearer inch by inch as they slid deeper into the furious gaping maw of the storm.

The wind grew stronger, and the howl in their ears was as a thousand mothers screaming in sorrow for ten thousand husbands, sons, and daughters lost at sea. And as the howl grew ever fiercer, the two came upon a mighty bed of reeds. The waves filled the air with a terrible acrid stench and tried to rip them from their seats; they used all their strength to hunker down so as not to be thrown clear of them into the air.

Kumo used this moment when paddling was impossible to ask, "ARE YOU CERTAIN THIS IS THE WAY!?" He had to scream to be heard.

"AYE, 'TIS NOT FAR NOW, BOY!" A terrible crash of thunder echoed on as Remora pointed quickly with one free hand and said, "JUST OVER YONDER IT WAITS!"

And so they struggled on. Throughout the sea of reeds, their mouths filled with the terrible taste of its rotting waters. They paddled now with unmatched vigor, until the current that carried them had grown so powerful that all their efforts were fruitless, and so instead they hung on for dear life, pulling out paddle and sword from the water, their destiny controlled by the torrent that swiftly carried them forward on its angry back.

They left the sea of reeds, greeted by what was almost surely land. Just rocks here and there at first, but then Kumo saw mangroves that whipped and bent as if under a terrible strain.

As they came closer to the mangroves, the sound of the wind tearing through them was utterly deafening. Branches lay bare, their leaves ripped ruthlessly from them, as each was bent unnaturally toward some central point—the same point, it would seem, to which Kumo and Remora's frail vessels were now being helplessly drawn with ever-increasing speed.

"BEHIND YOU!" Remora's warning came too late, only managing to make matters worse as Kumo turned just in time for the large mess of branches that flew at him to rip painfully across his face.

"WHAT NOW?!" Kumo felt sure that he was bleeding, but there was no time to worry about such trivial matters now, for bit by bit the vessels that carried them were being ripped apart.

"SORRY! NOT LONG NOW!"

"I KNOW! BUT WHAT THEN?! WH—" Kumo drew back in horror at what he saw next. A giant orb rose up out of the waters; its hue the blackest of blacks, it seemed to him to hold a pure and infinite emptiness. The reason the rivers ran backward now lay clear. For though the orb lay meters above them at its lowest point, the whole of the ocean was surging upward to meet and be consumed by it. An electrical hum, a buzzing, and many blue and white bolts spewed out from it, reaching far into the heavens and boiling the depths so that they bubbled and roiled.

As Kumo watched it—watched the orb steadily grow larger as it ate up the sea—he felt a sinking feeling inside himself, a sinking feeling made all the worse by the haste with which his tattered couch now dragged him toward its gaping, devouring mouth.

THE OSPREY

The ocean cradled *The Stranded One* in its cool embrace. There was a calmness in the air that was only interrupted by the faint sound of distant gulls and the soothing sound the sea made as it lapped gently against the vessel's glistening hull.

Time seemed to pass more slowly perched there above the depths that loomed deep below. The sea was so perfect, so calm and careless of the goings-on around it. If nothing else, Alice would miss the sea.

Soooo ... What exactly are we waiting for, again? You realize all this god-awful staring is unlikely to make him wake any faster? The voice in her head had been complaining for the last hour or so, but this was the first time she had really bothered to listen; though having heard his whining, she rather wished she had continued her efforts to tune him out.

Sigh. "What time is it, anyway?" Alice pulled away, her cheeks growing hot at the realization of exactly how close her face had come to Kumo's.

How should I know?! came his snide reply.

She had forgotten how offended he got at any mention of the time. The mere fact that she had forgotten this made her chuckle.

What?! If you wish to know so very much, why don't you ask your pet, what's-his-name!? Her bit of silent fun at his expense had done nothing to improve his temper, which made her smile.

"Hmm … Where is that boy, anyway? He should have come back by now." It had only just struck her … how long it had been since she had left Göttrick at the helm.

"We should be arriving shortly, after all." Were it anyone else's tardiness in question, this fact would be of little concern, but Göttrick in all his days had never once been late for anything without a very compelling reason.

Something I mentioned fifteen minutes ago … Not that you give a second thought to anything I have to say anymore. More whining, though it was not doubtful that he spoke the truth.

"Sorry," she lied, "I must have missed it."

Sure—whatever you say, princess. She could almost feel him trying to roll his eyes as he spoke.

Alice squeezed Kumo's hand in hers. And though she tried to pull away, she found her eyes betrayed her as they again lingered on the spot where he lay. It was several more awkward moments longer before she managed to close her eyes and pry herself from his side.

My god, woman! What has come over you? was her ever-insolent companion's reprimand, but she was numb to anything but the odd feeling that fluttered up from her stomach and through her arms.

She opened her eyes a moment too soon and bit her lip as she caught another fleeting glimpse of Kumo, but then her turn was made, and with some difficulty she pulled her dizzy frame to the cabin door.

She could almost feel the voice inside her shake his head as she went, and normally she would have made some attempt at a defense, but at the moment there were other matters to attend to.

ΔΔΔ

The ragged old tugboat bobbed leisurely on the open sea, like an oversized rubber shoe sloshing in a bucket of oil. Under new ownership, the tugger—formerly known as T-12 of the trash disposal fleet—had been recently renamed *The Osprey*.

Though she had never been well liked in her previous life, she found to her great joy and surprise that no matter what part of her happened to come out of alignment, no matter how worn her paint, no matter how deep the rust on her hull, her new master's love and care had not once faltered, not even on those not-so-rare-as-she-wished occasions when her will to move was lost entirely.

No, though burly and unkempt, her Bob was a good man, even a great man, in her perhaps somewhat biased opinion. A man who, however great in heart, unfortunately was born to parents who thought they were doing him a favor when they had chosen his name. "English is the next big thing, son!" they had told him whenever he asked "Why!?" It had been more like a cruel joke than a favor, though it was unlikely that they ever realized this—and he supposed he preferred it that way.

Sure, at times he had resented, hell, even hated them for it. But then on his 32nd birthday, in the middle of his usual rant about how terrible it was being the only Bob Kobayashi in the world, he was rudely interrupted by a four-year-old, one of his guests' children, no doubt. "Mister, why don't you just change your name?" The little girl, tenacious as any tot, floored Bob with those simple words, and though he had repeated her words sarcastically back to her—no doubt in some vain effort to regain some semblance of dignity—the thought stuck with him. It nagged at him for years: Why hadn't he just changed his name? Why had he stayed Bob Kobayashi, when he could be Akihiko Kobayashi, or Ebisu Kobayashi, or anything his heart desired? The question tore at him for years, nagging at him whenever he found himself looking in the mirror or trying to sleep. Several times he had even drafted plans to do it, to finally rid himself of the name he hated so much, but each time as he waited in line to turn in the papers, he simply could not bring himself to hand them over. It felt almost like a betrayal to him, one he could not bring himself to commit.

It was not until much later, while sitting at his father's deathbed, that he finally made peace with his "gift." "My son," his father said, "you have been a unique and wonderful gift to me in every way. I hope that our gift to you has brought you something different … something unique." His father's frail hands trembled in Bob's, and from that moment on, Bob's shame was gone. He was the one, the only Bob Kobayashi, and he had dedicated every day since to enjoying the life and name he had been given.

And so, as one thing led to another, Bob came into possession of the T-12, and though he was no fan of changing names, he had decided after some rather serious debate that she too deserved the gift he had been given. Ever since, they had spent much of their time together, Bob rambling on to her as they dredged up treasures from the depths below, and she listening quietly, making every effort she could to stay afloat—an effort she would likely not have made for any other captain.

Bob pulled the squeaky lever at his side, he had to disengage it twice, but to his relief it eventually pulled all the way back, locking into place. There was a clanking from the ship's bowels. *Must be a chain loose again*, he thought, as he watched their line slowly dragged out from the sea by the makeshift hoist arm he had managed to rig to *The Osprey*'s winch.

For a moment the rope slipped, and Bob was all but certain his prize would be lost to the sea, but the chain managed to just catch again before the rope was gone.

"Attagirl!" he said as he affectionately patted her controls—gently, of course, so as not to bring any misfortune upon them.

As the load she bore grew heavier, her whole right side was slowly lifted from the ocean's surface. Bob ran quickly from the helm to the awkward sprawl of welded rods that was *The Osprey*'s hoist arm, just managing to grab hold of the wriggling bulge of net and fish before she was over forty-five degrees to one side. Naturally, the moment he managed to pull the net his way, *The Osprey* crashed happily back to the water's surface.

There was a loud clank from below, and Bob barely jumped out of the way before the net came crashing to the very spot where he'd been standing. Upon impact, the net flew open, covering the whole deck in hundreds of fish who writhed lividly where they lay, their scales shining brightly in the afternoon sun.

"Ahh." He locked his hands behind his head and looked up to the heavens. "What a glorious day to be alive! Wouldn't you say, deario?"

Bob took a deep breath and began to sweep his catch into various holes that lined the deck. It was always so satisfying: the sound of dozens of fish plopping into the tanks below; the sound of a living, freshly caught.

Bob had always taken it as a good omen when only one thing broke on a catch, but he did not know what lay just behind him. After all, his was not the only ship out to make a catch in these waters.

DARK TITHE

She had not so much as made it to the door when there was a terrible crash and Alison found herself flung unexpectedly, and painfully, into it.

She was dazed for a moment by the unexpected blow to her head. Her heart raced, and she turned with bated breath, but all was well, at least as far as she was concerned. Broken and bandaged as he was, Kumo, it seemed, was none the worse for the unexpected crash that had sent half the contents of the room flying off their shelves. Indeed, the peaceful rise and fall of his chest seemed at odds with everything else about the poor boy and the many books and knickknacks that now littered the room around him.

Relieved, Alice let out a heavy sigh and took a long and angry breath through her nostrils as she tore open the cabin's door and stormed out toward the deck above.

At first there was no sound from above, but as she grew closer, she heard a frightened voice in the distance.

"P-Please! I'll d-do any-anything, s-sir!" so came the distant voice whose fear could be tasted in the air.

Clearly matters were worse than she had expected. Alison sprang lightly toward the light of day, her palms firmly upon the hilt of either blade.

There was a terrified scream—a scream cut suddenly short and replaced with a terrible silence.

She leaped out of the shadows, both blades at the ready, adrenaline making them eager for the taste of blood. But the deck that greeted her lay eerily devoid of any signs of struggle or of crew of any kind. The sight was so unexpected that for a moment she was unsure of what to do, her menacing blades swaying slightly from her heavy breathing as adrenaline coursed through her veins. Then she saw them, the ropes that hung from off the railings.

As she approached, the decrepit tugger over which her vessel now towered was revealed. This sight alone did nothing to surprise her, but what she saw next brought her blood to a boil.

On the deck below, if it could be called that, one of her men loomed ominously over a burly unkempt man, a man who quivered and cowered beneath the blade that threatened to quiet his "please."

No, sister! the voice in her head desperately screamed, *Be wary! Be still!* but his warnings came all too late. Alison, lost to her rage, had in an instant torn forward and now flew lightly through the air in a most graceful and terrifying display of her prowess.

ΔΔΔ

He hadn't expected to find himself here so soon. No, he had hoped for a little more time than this. Bob had always imagined things would have ended a little less suddenly, but here he found himself staring at the deck of his beloved *Osprey* for what seemed the last time.

He knew things weren't exactly going to plan when the big silver boat had slammed heartlessly into his poor girl's stern, but he had no idea how far from good things were until it was far too late.

The man, whose blade now burnt coldly across Bob's quivering neck, could scarcely have been seen boarding *The Osprey* before Bob had found himself in his current predicament. So far, the man, despite Bob's desperate pleas, had yet to utter a single word. Instead, each time Bob spoke, his assailant made sure to let his blade cut ever so slightly deeper into Bob's pasty flesh.

So, this is it, huh? I really expected a little more notice, Bob thought. *A girlfriend would have been nice, too, but I guess we had each other, dearie.* His eyes wandered over her deck as he thought fondly of the times they had spent together.

"He- ..." The blade pushed harder; he could feel the slow trickle of blood down his neck. *This won't do,* he thought. *How dare this vagrant deny me even my last words.*

Suddenly, Bob's silent fuming was interrupted by the sound of cloth whipping through the air in his direction. *I see. I am to be taken by another* was his thought as he peered up into the sun that was blotted out by the figure of the most vivacious female form he had laid eyes on in many a year. She flew toward him like an arrow and landed before him with unnerving grace as two harrowingly beautiful blades danced about her voluptuous frame.

"What is the meaning of this!" were the words belted forth from the angry soft lips of what it would seem was his black-haired heroine. Her eyes were narrowed, and her whole body rippled with an overwhelming disgust. He noticed the dried tears and blood all over her otherwise stark white gown, tears and blood that made her all the more enticing in a rare exotic way that Bob now regretted never before having learned to appreciate.

In fact, Bob found himself so hypnotized by her overwhelmingly erotic presence that he barely even noticed as the cold blade slid smoothly across his gullet.

As Bob found himself lying helplessly in the mounting evidence of his demise that now pooled around his right ear, he could not help but wonder briefly where the rest of him had gone. He even tried to ask a question to that effect but found himself, not surprisingly, voiceless.

Well, ain't that the darndest thing, he thought. *To think my biggest regret would be the unfortunate place I landed.* You see, Bob, in the process of losing his head, had landed in such a way that he had lost sight of her vivid presence. It was a presence that was so overwhelming that it seemed more important than his previous attachments (pun intended).

"You shall die for this treachery!" Had he anything left to get goosebumps on, Bob would have when he heard her voice exclaiming his imminent revenge.

How terribly unpleasant, Bob thought, as his inane attempts at inhalation caused him to feel only a terrible suffocating emptiness. *Now, Bob, let us not waste our last moments on silly habits like breathing*, he chided, trying to will the panic out of himself.

"I wouldn't do that, Dragon Lady. I am fairly certain we have some things you may be interested in keeping." The voice came from up above, just at the edge of Bob's vision. It was a man wearing a mask much like the one worn by the man who, some seconds earlier, had so generously freed Bob from all but a sliver of the torso that had been his burden to carry with him for a lifetime.

Bob heard her stop suddenly upon hearing the man's words. Bob held his breath in spite of himself, what little remained that is. It couldn't have been more than a moment later when many more masked faces appeared on the deck of the brilliantly silver silhouette of the other ship. To his ... up (formerly his right), they dangled the form of a man so heavily bandaged he was almost mummy-like in appearance. Strangely, more striking than the bandages was the brilliant silvery strands of hair that whipped in the wind as his body dangled almost as helplessly as Bob's own.

It was hard to discern the details of the commotion on the other ship's deck, but when Bob looked harder, he caught sight of a very different man who, despite his violent struggles, found himself almost equally helpless to deny the fate that had brought him to where he now hung. He was bound tightly with thick and unforgiving ropes that carried what appeared to be iron weights.

"Dragon Lady! You have not been yourself of late. We wish only that you answer one question, and we will gladly take whatever reparations you deem necessary."

The Dragon Lady, as it would seem she was called, said nothing. Things were starting to get blurry around the edges of Bob's vision, and he urged time to slow even more as he gazed out over the sea of red that now covered his beloved Osprey's modest decking.

"I ask you this, Dragon Lady. What is my name?" He said this with terrible authority in his voice and a surety it seemed he wished was not his own from the slight undertone that Bob's now-deft ears could pick out.

This time the Dragon Lady's pause was different; it seemed from the beat of her heart she was taken aback, perhaps surprised even.

This silence went on for some time. Until finally it was interrupted by the man who had brought it on. "Not even now?" he said, taking off his mask and revealing a man in what appeared his late forties, a man whose face now seemed so worn and dejected that even Bob felt a glimmer of sympathy when a single tear rolled down his cheek at the Dragon Lady's continued silence.

"You remember not the name you gave me? The boy you shaped into a man? The man who has served you loyally for a lifetime and would serve you loyally for a thousand more for but a name?" It seemed for a moment the man knew not what to do; clearly his resolve was lost for the moment.

The Dragon Lady's heart went on in beats of distress over those who dangled dangerously over the open ocean, or her apparent inability to locate the name she sought; Bob could not be entirely sure since things were getting a bit fuzzy on the edges by that point.

"Fine. Perhaps you have forgotten me, but surely you know the name of those you sent to certain doom earlier today?" This was his last attempt at perhaps convincing himself of her merit. "Surely this much you have kept." But, there was no confidence that this was the case in his wavering voice, which is the only reason one would have to say such a thing.

Now even Bob's ears were growing quiet, and as the silence carried on, his last thought was *You don't know it, do you, Dragon Lady ... That's too bad for you, I suppose. Too bad, indeed.*

"I see," he heard faintly whispered from somewhere in the distance. And, as two shadows fell slowly from where the silver chariot of death had been, they and Bob were at once no more.

TREADING WATER

Kumo and Remora had struggled for what seemed hours now against the raging waters that pulled them steadily closer to the terrible void that loomed ahead.

There was no limit to what the void could consume, no end to its destruction, no escape in sight. Kumo's arms tired of the constant battle to grip the rope that burned his palms as headway was made, then lost again and again.

Kumo's body, dodging debris in a futile effort to survive, was on autopilot; his mind was elsewhere. Remora's urgent commands had become an unintelligible murmur in the background. The end was almost here. He thought about what had led him to this point. Though he had expected to see his life flash before his eyes in this (slightly prolonged) final moment of life, he found himself lingering mostly on the times he had spent with Alison, brief though they may have been. He lingered on the touch of her fair skin; the smell of her lily perfume as it wafted off her elegant frame; the taste of her presence in the air wherever she'd been; the tears that marked the face of she, his savior, as her unwavering embrace carried him away from that place no nightmare could have prepared him to endure. Truly, his only regret would be not spending his last breaths again safe in her loving embrace.

Suddenly, there was a terrible lurching in Kumo's stomach, and the water that had once held him afloat was no more. Kumo was falling with ever-mounting speed until he crashed into the surface of the tide. Far above him, he could still see the dark void that now slowly consumed a dark rain cloud with ravenous fury.

And then Kumo made the immediately unpleasant discovery that his chair was missing when he found himself plunging into the watery depths. It took every fiber of his being to keep from succumbing to the reflex to breath as his whole body was immersed in the most frightfully frigid waters he had ever experienced. He tried frantically to swim but found that this was to no avail; he was sinking steadily, albeit slowly now, despite his furious efforts.

As the thrashing of his arms grew more frantic, Kumo saw Remora and his slowly sinking sofa in front of him. Remora did not look bothered in the least by the current state of things; as a matter of fact, he seemed, if anything, mildly entertained.

Kumo attempted to say something, but Remora quickly reached over and covered Kumo's mouth with his hand before anything could get out.

"My boy," Remora burbled as he stroked his chin inquisitively, "I do believe now to be a particularly intelligent time to wake." It was much like listening to a person trying to talk through a giant water-filled tuba.

"Bu-," again Kumo was muted by an agile hand. Kumo was confused—he was perfectly awake, ridiculously and painfully awake, in fact. Though he would not likely remain so for much longer, by his reckoning. It was already getting rather difficult to concentrate.

"I am sorry for this"—Remora didn't look too sorry, more like tickled pink, Kumo thought—"but it appears this is the only way."

Before Kumo could react, he met with the unpleasant force of Remora's enthusiastic fist as it found its way square into the middle of Kumo's now-bewildered face.

When he opened his eyes a moment later, he found himself in the same place, perhaps it was a little darker now, but alone. He made to continue his thrashing, and then it hit him, the terrible pain that coursed through every inch of his cold and frightened body—the body that now failed to respond to his command to move. Well, it had perhaps moved an inch, but no more.

He continued to will his limbs to move, but he had no control of them. He was helpless. This really did seem to be the end.

ΔΔΔ

Despite all that was invested in Kuve, Alice still found herself heading to Göttrick first as she plunged into the depths of the icy cold waters. It didn't take her long to find him, and it took her even less time to free him as she pushed him into one of the many large tires that lined *The Osprey*'s hull.

Now she searched frantically for the boy, not seeing him anywhere. A terrified frantic desperation was growing inside her.

You fool! I told you, did I not?! The voice was ripe with fresh anger, and Alice wasn't sure if it was because of her interests or his own.

"Now is not the time!" She needed to concentrate. She needed to look for any sign of him, anything that could help her find him ... but there was nothing ... nothing, save a vast and empty blackness that seemed to stretch endlessly before her. She needed to breath, but she refused to come up for air. She would rather die now than give him up to the sea, a realization that truly baffled her slowly numbing mind.

Onward she trod through the bleak dark depths that grew heavy around her until she finally found herself slowing as the last of the air in her lungs bubbled forth. She stared out into the darkness, wondering how close she would be to him when they'd both settled to the sea's floor. She lingered a moment longer in consciousness to wish for just one more touch before the end. By then, even the voice had grown quiet. Nothing was left but darkness.

And so, they both drifted in the dark cold embrace of the unforgiving sea that had swallowed them whole, unaware of how close to each other they now lay. In fact, for a time, were they conscious, they could have reached out and their hands would have touched in the depths of the abyss.

But their hands stirred not as the currents momentarily brought them together. For but an instant, a blinding light engulfed them both. The ocean was lit like the sun-filled sky, and for less than the blink of an eye, it was as a brilliant krill-filled snow globe. Then, that fleeting moment having passed, darkness once more filled the ocean's depths as the very forces that had brought them together now tore them apart. Their lifeless forms drifted helplessly, ever farther from one another.

COLD EMBRACE

As Kumo opened his eyes, Alice was as an angel before him. Her skin was pale and perfect as the dim light washed across her in beautiful waves. Her long white dress floated gently about her elegant form and billowed softly behind her. He edged closer. She was so quiet, so still. Her black hair danced across her face, but her form remained motionless.

He lifted his thin fingers toward her cheek and noticed for the first time the bandage that clung to it. There was little light where they were, but he could see the blood that stained the bandages. *This is no dream* was his frantic thought, a thought that came with a sudden rush of pain and a terrible need for air that he hadn't felt before.

He wrapped his arms around her and demanded that they pull his angel to safety but found no strength in them; he told his legs to kick, but they responded not.

He was powerless, and all he could do was press his lips upon her cold forehead and shed one last tear into the vast sea.

He felt the water filling his lungs, but he was careful to concentrate on the touch of her skin against what little of his remained exposed. As his lungs filled, he was overcome by a terrible heaviness. But soon that heaviness released its grip on him, and for a moment, his world was just Alice— his being was suffused with what he, in that moment, realized could be only his love for her.

The beauty of that moment was seized from him when he felt himself being torn from her side. As the force of the water carried him away, there was nothing left for him but the depths of emptiness and despair. As he drifted farther and farther from his love, he even lost the terror that had been consuming him since he'd awoken. His struggle was over; he welcomed the darkness. Maybe it would set him free.

Perhaps, somewhere in the darkness, he could find her again. Perhaps, in the darkness, he would be freed from the terrible pain of separation and loss. The darkness grew stronger, and, though he welcomed it, he spent one last moment picturing her radiant smile before giving himself up to it.

Now all was quiet, calm, empty. There was no pain, no sadness, no memories, no desires, no hopes, no dreams. There was no need for such things. What needs do the dying and the dead have for these? At the end of the terrible struggle called life, a man is fortunate if he discovers the comfort to be had in a peaceful and quiet mind.

Kumo could have spent the time he had left questioning, regretting, fighting, but instead he was content to savor the purity of silence of mind, body, and soul.

ΔΔΔ

Göttrick watched the water intently as he ripped the mask from his face and removed the straps from his armor. His fingers shook from the chill that made the simple task a laborious one. From aloft *The Osprey* he heard piercing laughter.

"Leave them to their fates, men! We have gained what we set out to obtain."

The crew was silent until the traitor uttered the words "Our futures!" The last thing Göttrick heard as he dove into the dark depths was the sound of the mob's cheers in response.

The cold that surrounded him made it hard to hold his breath, and the darkness of the water obscured his view. He searched frantically for any sign of his mistress. No clue appeared to give him hope, so he swam down farther.

Nothing! He returned to the surface quickly and inhaled deeply before returning to his search. Over and over, he dove into the depths, until he lost all hope.

She must be here somewhere, he thought as he dove one last time. He quietly floated in the depths and scanned the waters beneath him. *All is lost, you fool,* he despaired, but, as he began his return to the surface, out of the corner of his eye he saw a bright flash of light amidst the darkness below.

Could it be ...? He did not pause to finish the thought, instead he turned and swam with all the ferocity that was left in him to the source of what now was the faintest of glows in the distance.

The hissing in his ears pained him as the pressure around him grew steadily greater, but his only thought was of Alice, who was now almost within arm's reach. The strange glow seemed to emanate from Kumo's limp hand, which drifted slowly away from Alice's sickeningly still figure.

With what little energy he had left, Göttrick wrapped his strong fingers gingerly around her cold pale arm and began to drag her with all his might to the surface. It was with no small sense of pleasure that he thought simply to pass Kumo's outstretched glowing palm.

She will have to understand that I could save only her, he thought, but then the image of her tears filled his vision, and against his better judgment, he placed an unnecessarily tight grip over Kumo's wrists and began the struggle to the surface.

It seemed an age had passed in the depths below, but eventually Göttrick found the relief of the surface. He gasped for the air he so desperately needed, and as he dragged his burden to the small dingy, he found the color slowly returning to his vision. He realized that he had been closer to remaining with them in the depths below than he had thought, but then all that filled his mind was dread as he painfully dragged himself and the two he carried onto the stern of The Osprey.

As he struggled to bring them up with him, he was very thankful for the tires that covered the sides of the ship. With some effort, he finally found himself kneeling before the two bodies that lay perfectly and horribly still in cold wet puddles that pooled beneath them.

Adrenaline surged through his veins as he frantically pumped against her still frame in an attempt to revive her. As he pumped and blew air into her water-filled lungs, he felt the tears run down his face as hope once again turned to despair.

ΔΔΔ

The peaceful silence in her mind was abruptly disrupted when Alice felt a terrible burning sensation filling her throat and lungs. She felt her chest pounding with an unnatural fury, and though she tried, she could not take a breath. Her eyes were open, but she saw nothing but a hazy blur as she felt salty water and blood pouring out of her mouth.

She thought for a moment that she saw Göttrick as her body writhed and convulsed, but moments later her vision was filled with darkness again.

ODDLY ALIVE

Some time had passed when the air grew unexpectedly sweet as it swept through her nostrils. *The air!* she exuberantly exclaimed (in her head, of course, since she hadn't quite decided to wake yet).

As she felt the air coursing through her lungs, she methodically catalogued each and every identifiable scent. Though she smelled a faint sweetness, it was mostly the smell of mud that struck her ... *salty, stinking mud, and ... is that seaweed?*

It was at that moment that she was stirred from her peaceful slumber by the methodical ripple of the mud beneath her. Try though she did, the longer she ignored it, the deeper she sank, as each tremor sent wet mud rushing over her arms.

As she finally gave in and opened her eyes, she was overwhelmed by the bright noonday sun. She felt slimy muck between the fingers of one hand, while the other hand was experiencing an entirely different sensation. She felt a familiar hand in hers, but it was cold, much too cold. She sat up with a start and stared in surprise at the limp and motionless body beside her. Kumo lay lifeless in the mud.

What happened next Alice did not understand and she had no explanation for. She could see that Kumo's chest was moving, but seemingly not of his own volition. His flesh had a blue pallor to it. Her hand under his nostrils felt no air passing, and his mouth was closed. This, and the unexplained pulsations of the ground around him, sent chills down her spine. She tightened her grip on his hand and knelt over him. In her desperation, she joined the unknown force that thrust hard upon Kumo's lifeless chest.

She tried to fill his lungs with air from her own, but her breath met heavy resistance. She reached her fingers into his throat, but there was nothing inside blocking his airway. Whatever was causing the resistance, it seemed to be another thing she couldn't see. Desperately, she continued to pound upon his chest; desperately, she pressed and blew until long after even the unseen force had ceased its own attempts at resuscitation.

ΔΔΔ

Kumo had emptied himself, piece by piece. This would be his final chore, he thought. And it was, for a time, until something he had rid himself of came back unexpectedly. He suddenly felt a terrible pain … a pain from someplace that felt more like all over.

And then it all came rushing back: every ache and pain, every memory good and bad returned with a sudden and painful rush as, jerking upward, he choked on a lungful of salt water in the most shockingly painful breath of his life. In that same moment, his eyes shot open, and it was all he could do not to scream as the bright sunlight burnt through the darkness that had filled them.

The world suddenly began to pour back in around him. All that met his eyes was a terrible and overwhelming brightness, and all he felt was a cold and oppressive heaviness in all his limbs.

"Kuve!" He had only just recognized her voice when he felt Alice wrap painfully around him. He felt her warm lips pressed hard against his own as her image slowly came into focus before him. Tears streaked down her cheeks as she held him in a passionate embrace he thought would never end.

He took a deep breath as her lips left his. Everything was getting less fuzzy, and colors were starting to get brighter. Alice pulled him painfully upright and now held him firmly in her arms.

"I thought I had lost you!" Her breath was labored, and she shivered violently as she pressed him to her chest. He felt her heart beating hard through the wet clothing they both wore, and as she held him closely, he saw mangroves rising up behind her. Their branches rose so high above the two that they blotted out all but small fragments of the sky. The thick mud at his feet seemed to almost gently flow as it burbled its way to the deeply obscured path ahead.

"Wha—" he attempted to speak, but the pain in his chest grew almost instantly unbearable.

Alice met his gaze and shook her head with concern just before wrapping her delicate fingers around his head and resting her lips upon the top of his brow. "Don't you ever do that to me again. Ever," she whispered.

There was a long silence as they both felt their bodies warmed slowly by the midday sun that had already begun to dry their cold wet clothes.

"Don't worry, Kuvey, I'll get us out of here," she whispered softly as she held his head gently upon her breasts.

Though, I must confess, I've no clue where here *is,* she thought as she shook her head and slowly scanned her surroundings to find a path to higher ground.

Though it caused him much pain, Kumo wrapped his arms around her and stammered, "Ho-How did you get here?" Alice could barely hear his voice against the many sounds that filled the air as the creatures in the mangroves sang and croaked all around them.

"Here? Do you know where we are?" Alice pulled away just enough to gaze into his eyes. His exhaustion showed on his face. "How did we get here, Kuve?" she pled as he gathered what little strength he had to muster a response.

It was some time before he felt the waves of pain beginning to subside within him, and even longer before he found himself able to softly speak. "I don't know how you got here. Actually, I don't know how I got here, either, but I'm pretty sure that I've been there before." He pointed to a swirling blackness that was just barely visible in the distance.

She slowly turned her head to meet the object of his attention. She had been so focused on their immediate surroundings that she had barely even noticed the cracking sounds that issued from somewhere in the distance. But now her gaze was drawn to the swirling mass of darkness that seemed to pulse and writhe as the neighboring mangroves were ripped ruthlessly from their roots and consumed by it in an instant.

"What on earth is that?!" she exclaimed, doing a poor job of hiding her apprehension.

"It's somewhat different from how it was before," Kumo shrugged, "but if it's all the same to you, I would like to avoid going there again."

THE SEA OF SOLITUDE

Though Göttrick could hear that Alison's breathing was labored (but given that she was, at least, breathing), he thrust frantically upon her companion's blood-soaked chest with relentless dedication. All the while, save for her rasping breath, Alison remained motionless some distance away. Göttrick had placed her as far as he could from the puddle of blood that was still slowly spreading from atop the deck's hatch where its former captain had fallen.

Breath after breath, Göttrick pushed air into Kumo's lungs, but the sickly tone of Kumo's skin did not change; try though he might, Göttrick could not manage to get the boy to start breathing again. Göttrick wasn't very familiar with the procedures needed to deal with this situation and really regretted not having paid more attention to them during his training.

Göttrick felt Kumo's ribs breaking beneath his palms as he thrust for what seemed a thousand years, but it was all to no avail thus far. He wanted so badly to tend to his mistress, but he could still hear her ragged breath, so he knew she had some time yet and would not forgive him if he did not do everything in his power to try to save the one before him.

Finally, it came to the point, as Kumo's blood slowly coated Göttrick's fingers, that the cracking below him felt more like a desecration than an attempt to save a life.

Göttrick stared in a disquieted haze as the blood that covered the deck slowly trickled off *The Osprey* and clouded the open seas behind them in thick red clouds that were already bringing the sharks from far and wide. Their fins danced back and forth as they made their frenzied search for the feast they smelled.

Standing in dismay at the edge of the ship's bow, he pushed the former captain's head and torso overboard into the sea while he tried to clear his mind. He did not watch, but he heard, the hungry, circling creatures that had been summoned by the steady trickle of blood overboard, ripping the corpse apart with frenzied vigor.

The pain of defeat consumed him; he knew the grief that would fill her heart and longed for the power to have prevented its cause, but there was nothing else to be done.

He turned to tend to Alison and was caught completely by surprise when he realized that she had somehow managed to make her way from the other side of the deck to Kumo's side. She lay next to the boy, gripping his cold dead hand tightly in her own. Seeing her hand on his filled him with a wave of relief, relief that was immediately followed by terrible remorse for his inability to save the boy's life.

Göttrick closed his eyes and took a deep breath before opening his eyes again and checking that Alison was okay. Her breathing had become more regular, but she shivered furiously and murmured desperately; he couldn't make out her words. Her skin, though less pale now, still had a slight blue hue to it around her lips and eyelids that made Göttrick rather uneasy. He had never seen his mistress this vulnerable. He had cared for her when her intoxication had left her unable to walk or even caused her to pass out, but there was a distinct difference between that and her current state.

He clambered to his feet and dashed down the hall, throwing open each door he passed until he finally came to the captain's quarters. To his relief, there was a small bed in the cabin that had clean dry bedding. Grabbing the bedding, he turned in a flash and made his way back to his lady's side.

Göttrick paused as he approached the miserable heap of a man whom he had failed to save and his lady's wet and ragged form beside him. Her hand was still wrapped tightly around Kumo's and her lips now moved silently as the two lay in a bloody pool that reflected the late afternoon sunlight in a way that was a little disturbing.

He stared, paralyzed by curiosity, as her grip tightened over Kumo's limp hand. He felt a terrible sadness fill his soul, for in her current state she could not know that the boy was gone.

All he had ever wanted was to make her smile, easy and carefree. All he had ever wanted was to bring his mistress the happiness that always seemed to elude her. And now that she had finally found it, he had failed to keep it from slipping through her fingers.

He had always wished that he would be enough for her, but it was, sadly, not his place to bring peace to her life, not his place to be any more to her than what he already was.

Alone again, he was sure, she would return to the drinking that was so destructive, and the small light of hope that had recently warmed her would be extinguished, perhaps forever.

As tears streamed down her cheeks and her incoherent murmurs grew ever more urgent, suddenly the boy's back arched and his chest pressed rhythmically in a disturbingly unnatural way. Göttrick was paralyzed, not knowing what to do, until the boy suddenly stopped thrashing on the deck and sputtered bloody water from his cold, and formerly dead, lips.

The spell that had fallen over him broken, Göttrick rushed to Alison's side and tried to lift her from the deck to wrap her in the bedding he had brought from the captain's cabin. Try though he did, he could not pry her hand from Kumo's, and now he worried that he might cause further injury if he tried to move them. Already, he could hear a terrible crunching sound every time the boy took a breath.

He tried to get as much of their wet clothing off as he could, but he still couldn't pry their hands apart. He once again pulled as hard as he felt comfortable and stopped when he felt he might be doing more harm than good. *God, she is strong.* Finally, giving up entirely on the idea of separating them, he cut Alison's dress with his tanto blade and pulled it off while doing his best to avert his eyes. He tried to wipe up as much blood as he could before gingerly slipping sheets and blankets first under and then around them both.

Eventually, both of them were breathing regularly, and all her murmuring and shivering had ceased. The emergency handled as best he could for the moment, Göttrick trained his eyes on the seas before them, seas that, upon further inspection, were empty, save for a black dot that bobbed from swell to swell with unchecked speed straight to the place where *The Osprey* lay perched upon its salty nest.

A rush of fresh terror filled him, and he ran up the stairs to the wheelhouse. To his dismay, despite her current snail-like pace, *The Osprey*'s motors were, in fact, already running at full speed. He tried desperately to push the throttle forward farther, but it was to no avail.

Giving up hope of an escape, Göttrick ran to the deck and drew his blades to defend his mistress. It was not long before two familiarly masked figures had made it within clear sight of *The Osprey*. They boarded the vessel from the small black rubber boat that earlier had served as the beacon decoy for *The Stranded One*. Though Göttrick disliked the thought of open battle with his former brothers-in-arms, he was relieved that it was, at least, only two of them. The men approached from over the ship's stern.

I suppose I couldn't have expected it to be any more difficult for them to board than it was for me, he thought, as he realized the convenience of the tire-covered hull was an obvious double-edged sword. Of course, that was probably not the only trait of the vessel that made her less than battle worthy.

"Stand down, Göttrick!" the man nearest him shouted with his hand upon the hilt of his katana. "What is the meaning of this display!?"

"Hold your tongue, you traitorous scum! You will not touch our mistress!" Göttrick's deep loathing was obvious in his tone.

"What madness has overcome you? What have you done to the Dragon Lady?!" The second masked figure drew his blade as he confirmed that it was his mistress that lay unconscious behind Göttrick on the still very obviously blood-soaked deck.

The man approached Alison's helpless form, and without thinking, Göttrick turned his back on the man in front of him to rush the man who threatened his mistress. In an instant, he found himself pinned to the ground by his assailants and his blades ripped expertly from his hands. No one had ever managed to disarm him, save for the Dragon Lady herself—until now, that was. Then again, he never would have thought his brothers would mutiny or that he would see a dead man resume breathing. He seemed to be living in a different world of late; it would take him a while to catch up to this new reality.

A boot landed hard upon his hand, sending a crushing pain up his arm. "I ask again: What have you done to the Dragon Lady?" His assailant pressed a blade into Göttrick's gullet. "Speak or die, scum!"

"This is what you planned, wasn't it?" Göttrick gasped.

The man let up slightly on his blade to allow Göttrick to speak.

"Well, I am sorry I was unwilling to simply watch them die as you would have had me do."

They listened silently, unsure of the meaning of his words.

"How dare you now ask such questions?!"

"What on earth are you talking about, Göttrick? We have only just returned." As he spoke, he removed his sword from Göttrick's neck altogether and pulled him to his feet.

"Where has everyone else gone? Where is the crew?"

"You-You really do not know?" Göttrick shook his head in disbelief. "Khalo has mutinied and taken the ship. Everyone else has joined him. How could you not have known?"

"We were not aboard the ship, but at sea. How can so much have come to pass in such a short time?"

"I had thought the order was lost entirely. We were dropped into the sea and left for dead by those foul defectors." Göttrick wiped away some blood from his neck.

"Um ... Sorry," said the man who had held the katana to his neck. "We had no way of knowing."

"What's done is done. If, indeed, you are not traitors, then make haste. We must get this vessel to port if there is any hope that we will survive. We cannot depend upon knowledge of our mistress's survival nor her vulnerable state remaining secret. We must assume our enemies will continue pursuit and be ready for them." His command had barely issued forth before the two men scattered in solemn obedience to attend to The Osprey's seaworthiness.

They slowly advanced across the open sea toward the green island that peeked over the horizon. Night descended upon them as Göttrick watched Alice's and Kumo's chests rise and fall reassuringly. With each of their breaths taken, he collected another little drop of hope that they might survive their injuries. Though he could do nothing to explain how the boy now lived, it was a relief that he would not have to explain his failure to the Dragon Lady when she woke.

For now, the calm and reassuring sounds of the sea surrounded them, but this comfort likely would not last long. Only time could tell what awaited them when they came ashore.

THANK YOU

Thank you so much for joining me on this amazing journey! I hope you enjoyed reading this story as much as I enjoyed creating it. If you liked this book, then you will love "Nemia Rising: The Dig," a foray into Kumogami's youth and a worthwhile read, and of course the next book in this series is in the works. Check out nemiarising.com/next to get access to the next book in the series as soon as it is available.

I have spent many, many years of my life working on this masterpiece, and honestly, without the help of my friends, family, and editors (many of whom are the same), this book would never have been possible. So, let me take another moment to thank anyone who had a hand in convincing me to stop fussing about perfection and to finally pull the trigger on publishing.

Be sure to join my email list (please go to: nemiarising.com/next) to be the first to know when the next book in the series has been released and to get early discounted pricing on anything else I write in the future.

If you enjoyed this book and have the time to share your experience with other readers in the form of a review, it would go a long way toward making it possible for me to continue to dedicate the long hours, and to purchase the many cups of coffee, it takes to create these worlds for you. I dream of the day that I can dedicate more of my time to being an author, and I appreciate your help in making that dream a reality.

I know you are ready to dive deeper and experience more of Kumogami's adventures, so be sure to get on the mailing list so you don't miss out when I have finished another episode.

The world of Nemia Rising is full of mysteries that even I, its creator, have yet to unlock, but, as we journey together, you and I, I know its secrets will reveal themselves to us.

Again, for the latest, head to nemiarising.com/next. I look forward to experiencing the next leg of this adventure with you soon!

www.ingramcontent.com/pod-product-compliance
Lightning Source LLC
Chambersburg PA
CBHW052045240626
47153CB00006B/2216